The Renegade

The Renegade

Lauran Paine

Thorndike Press • Chivers Press
Thorndike, Maine USA   Bath, Avon, England

This Large Print edition is published by Thorndike Press, USA
and by Chivers Press, England.

Published in 1995 in the U.S. by arrangement with
The Golden West Literary Agency.

Published in 1995 in the U.K. by arrangement with the
Author, c/o The Golden West Literary Agency.

U.S. Hardcover   0-7862-0396-X   (Western Series Edition)
U.K. Hardcover   0-7451-3028-3   (Chivers Large Print)
U.K. Softcover   0-7451-3032-1   (Camden Large Print)

The text of this Large Print edition is unabridged.
Other aspects of the book may vary from the original edition.

Set in 16 pt. News Plantin by Warren Doersam.

Printed in Great Britain on permanent paper.

British Library Cataloguing in Publication Data available

Library of Congress Cataloging in Publication Data

Paine, Lauran.
    The renegade / Lauran Paine.
        p.   cm.
    ISBN 0-7862-0396-X (lg. print : hc)
    1. Large type books.   I. Title.
[PS3566.A34R45   1995]
813'.54—dc20   94-45643

The Renegade

Chapter One

The room had thousands of fly specks on its grey walls that had once been whitewashed. It was a small, bare place but for a scarred old table and five captain's-chairs, and three men standing looking at the one man who was sitting. Of the standing men, the shortest, squattest, was evidently the one whose words carried the most weight. He had his nickel circlet with its star inside the circle pinned carelessly on his shirt. A lawman who wore his authority easily because he'd worn it so long. Grey, seamed, with blue eyes hidden behind a perpetual squint, he smoked a cigarette with slow acceptance, as though one usually hung from his face.

"Like to hear what you have to say, Williams," the sheriff said quietly, his eyes never leaving the sitting man's face, nor blinking.

The man called Williams was in his early thirties. He had a look of hard-packed physical power. It was in the bunched-up thickness of his shoulders, the full flatness of his chest and in the mighty turn of his neck. But his skin showed shiny sweat, like an overlay, lying upon the sun-burnt, deep, rich colouring of his face. He was patently having trouble staying in the chair. His hands gave him away. Obviously he wanted to stand up, to walk around the room like a caged bear, but he didn't.

"I was in the shop. There were some tugs had to be sewn for the stage company. We're behind, anyway, and they're short of tugs. I told Will I'd finish one set of them, anyway."

"Did you finish 'em?"

Williams nodded. "Yes."

The sheriff was thoughtfully silent for a moment; then he shifted his weight, stood hipshot and attentive. "And you didn't hear anything at all? Town's pretty quiet late at night, Dexter."

"No," Williams said, "I didn't hear a sound."

One of the two deputies, a tall, angular man with a hatchet face and intolerant eyes, snorted: "Wall's not more'n three inches thick."

The sheriff glanced once, fleetingly, at his deputy, then ignored him. "Didn't hear a holler, even?"

"Nothing," Dexter Williams said stubbornly, but his hands were holding to his knees and their palms were clammy with oily sweat.

8

"Not a sound, sheriff. If I had, I'd of told you."

The other deputy walked to a chair and sat down with a sigh. His bootsteps had made dull, unnecessarily loud echoes and his spur rowels rang musically. He was built along the same lines as the sheriff. In fact, he was Eb Bulow, Sheriff Tom Bulow's son.

"Listen, Dexter," the younger Bulow said in a voice almost as quiet and controlled as his father's, "look at it like this. You were in the saddle shop. You say so yourself. Right next door is the stage company's office. They had nine thousand in bullion in their safe and a guard over it. Someone slipped in the back window, knocked the guard out and crowbarred the safe open, took the money and beat it. Now, don't it seem likely a man close to all this, as you say you were, would've heard *some* noise?"

Dexter Williams felt the hopelessness of his situation. It pressed in around him from three sets of eyes. The little room itself was redolent of a sourness that was old sweat from others who had sat as he was sitting. And yet he hadn't heard anything the night before. Nothing; not a single solitary sound of any kind. Nor had he left the shop, but the oppressive sense of guilt was in him just the same. Innocent, he didn't feel that way, and he knew why, too. A man who once served a jolt in prison was bound to feel that way. It was part of the stigma that went with an ex-convict for ever. Dexter hadn't known it before, but he knew it now.

It made him feel helpless, as though he were tongue-tied. Like a man under water trying to shout. Nothing he could say would erase the steady suspicion that shone out of three sets of eyes. He wanted fresh air of a sudden. To be able to walk and walk and walk, head down; walk the crawling futility out of his system. Instead, he had to act the part of sincerity, and while he *was* telling the truth, he knew they didn't believe him. So he was acting his part without being convincing about it, and he knew that, too.

"Sheriff, I can't tell you any more than I have. I was in the shop. I didn't hear anything. That's all."

Tom Bulow went to a chair and dropped into it. Only the tall, lean, hostile deputy was still standing now. "Well, Dexter," he said not unkindly, "like Eb said. Don't it seem funny you wouldn't have heard something?"

"Yes." The smoke-grey eyes had an eloquence moving in depths that Dexter Williams couldn't form into words.

"But you didn't," Tom Bulow said, quietly.

"I didn't."

The lean deputy snorted. "You was pretty stubborn on that horse stealin' charge, too, wasn't you?"

Dexter's head moved around so that he could look squarely into the unfriendly man's face. "That was a long time ago. I was a kid then."

"Sometimes they don't ever —"

"That'll do, Slim," the sheriff said, but Dexter knew the rest of it all right; it wasn't the first time he'd heard it, and probably wouldn't be the last time, either. Maybe that was what was in the minds of the two impassive, thoughtful Bulows. Once an outlaw always an outlaw.

It was borne down upon him like a hot iron that no hot-blooded kid could know what the cost was of getting caught in a crime. If they did know, they wouldn't commit the crimes.

He looked at the fly-specked wall. Wouldn't they? Sure they would. He'd had a vague idea of what would happen, and yet he'd gone ahead and stolen the horse. No; it was one of those things that no kid is ever smart enough to understand. Age has to show them, like it did Dexter Williams, and by that time the stain wouldn't wash out.

On an instinct he stood up, reached for his tobacco and began to make a cigarette; knew it was a mistake as soon as he'd troughed the

11

paper, because his hands were shaky and three sets of eyes saw them like that.

Sweating harder, he bulled it through, anyway, lit and exhaled. He was a medium-sized, powerfully-built man with a handsome set of eyes, a good mouth that was firm above a square chin, and a nose that was broad enough to detract from the curse of too-prominent, high cheekbones.

Sheriff Tom Bulow studied him in detached silence. Dexter Williams was all man even without a gun, and that, more than anything else, stamped him an ex-convict. No gun athwart his hips in a land where no man went without one unless the law forbid him to wear one, like it did in this case.

"Dex. Do me a favour. When you go back to the shop, ask Will if he'll step up here."

Williams looked at the sheriff through a blue tendril of smoke. It didn't sound right. "I can go?" he asked, afraid to believe it.

"Yeah."

So Dexter went back out into the early morning sunlight and stood on the scuffed, colourless duckboards that ran along before the stores of Lovell, Arizona Territory, and smoked his cigarette. Lovell wasn't much more than a clutch of weathered, warped buildings leaning defensively on one another against the twin scourges of the far frontier:

12

wind and sun. It was a cowtown and all that denoted, which meant mercantile establishments, liverybarns; places like The Drover's Rest, a cafe sandwiched between other false-fronts, the Green Springs Stage and Transfer Company, and four saloons.

The Green Springs Stage and Transfer Company office had a few stragglers standing out front under the overhang, talking. He saw them and winced inwardly from thought of what — and whom — they were discussing. Then he dropped the cigarette and went down the way toward Will Herndon's Harness Shop, knowing the men would see him, but keeping his head down just enough so that he wouldn't be forced to see them; to speak, maybe, and get that impersonal, look-through-you glance he'd run across before, years back.

Once he looked up. That was when a slow-walking rider with big Chihuahua spurs went by him. He knew the spurs and the man. Had played poker with him in the dingy, entirely masculine world that was the Con Brown Saloon. It was a fleeting glance; then they were past; but the sardonic, almost cynical look in the other man's face had been enough. Dexter hadn't spoken. They moved away from each other in total silence.

Will Herndon looked up when Dex came through the door. He kept his glance on the younger man's face until Dex hung his hat on the buckhorn rack and faced him; then the doe-soft brown eyes, that belied completely the stormy disposition of their owner, blinked. What Herndon said was almost ridiculous, and therefore showed that the harness shop owner hadn't thought it out in advance.

"Glad you finished those tugs last night, Dex."

The bland ludicrousness of it hit Dexter hard. He looked at Will for a second, then chuckled. And all at once he felt the coiled-up tenseness in his chest dissolve as though it had never been there. "Yeah. Did they come for them, Will?"

"Noooo," Herndon drawled, dropping his glance to the saddleskirt he was stitching in the upright jaws of a sewinghorse, "I took 'em over."

"Sure," Dexter said, understanding Will's desire to know things. He moved through the atmosphere of the shop, breathing deeply of the leather smell, feeling the security it always inspired in him, and loving it just like he loved the leather he worked with every day, and sometimes until late at night as well. "The sheriff wants you to come up, Will."

Herndon's limpid, incongruously-beautiful eyes came up, held to Dexter's face a moment, then he dropped the dual needles and leaned both arms on the jaws of the sewinghorse. "All right," he said in that deceiving voice of his. "What's on his mind? You know?"

"No; but I've got an idea. I'm probably wrong, but I suspect he'll want to know if I've been working nights lately — stuff like that."

"Oh!" Will backed off the horse, unconsciously brushed at non-existent sheep's wool that might have come off the saddleskirt, and stood erect. At forty-five or so he was just beginning to grey above the ears. He had a formidable jaw and a hard mouth, with an upward quirk at the corners. Laughter wrinkles that were neutralised by vertical, deep lines between his eyebrows at the high pinch of his nose, showing that his face could mottle over quickly with black storminess. He was a man of contrasts, Dexter knew. So did Lovell know it, for Will Herndon had lived there many years. Intensely loyal, fun loving, he was also violent in his angers.

"I'll go on up, Dex." But he made no move to pick up his black hat, cleared his throat instead and ran one hand, the left one, through the matt of black hair he was crowned with. "Dex?"

"Yes?" The smoke-grey eyes swung to the brown ones, waiting.

15

"Did you do it?"

"No."

A moment of silence, then Will felt for the black hat, dumped it unceremoniously on his head, and turned away. "Be back directly. Watch things, huh?"

"Sure."

Dexter watched him go, thinking that in Will Herndon's lithe, quick way of moving was the real key to the man's personality. His mind went back six months with a flashback of the three years before that, when he'd been convicted as a horse thief and sent to Territorial Prison.

He had served the years because he'd had to. If it had been possible to break out he'd have done it the first two years, but the last one was a time of maturing for a wild waif who had known no home or ties since he could remember. Somewhere, down the line of the inheritance he knew nothing of, someone had bequeathed him a legacy of good, common sense, but it had been late in manifesting itself. Not until that last year; then he'd forgotten the fierce hope for impossible escape. How impossible, he didn't find out until the day he was called up for release; the old warden, a dyspeptic, ruthless man with clipped speech and eyes like glacial ice, had talked bluntly about the prison and the life beyond it for those who had paid the debt to a society that was, as yet, sparse enough on the frontier.

"Williams," he had said, "you were a wild 'un when you came here. We had two men watching you from inside. I'm glad you got hold of yourself. I hate sneaks just like you or anyone else does, but here we got to have them. See out there? See those beautiful headboards? Those were the ones who didn't know about our inside spy system. They didn't all die of yellow jack. Well, forget that; it's behind you. And listen to me a minute, then you can go. You've paid up for horse stealing, and I'm glad. Maybe you don't believe me, but I am. I'm glad for every bucko who walks out of here. Only time I'm off 'em is when they come back the second time. I hope you don't, Williams. You'd better not. You don't want my advice, I don't reckon, but you're going to get it, anyway. If you met any boys in here, forget 'em. If you've got old friends outside, forget them, too. Break clean, Williams, and start over clean. Don't ever go back where you've been. If you do, it'll be hard for you. It'll be hard for you, anyway, so don't make it any harder. You had seventeen dollars when you came here. There it is. The gun you'll never get back, and from now on it's against the law for you to wear one. Remember that. Don't pack a gun, Williams!" Then he had stood up, the hard, bent core of a man old and acid in face and disposition, and held out a claw-like hand. "Good luck, boy." ₂

Dexter had walked seven miles to the first town. The mantle of freedom after three years of close, smelly confinement was strange on him, like the ill-fitting clothes he wore. A stranger to himself he had been, but not a vengeful one. And in that first town he had seen the wise, knowing winks when he walked past. Even heard a few not so softly spoken slurs. He'd kept on going, afraid to risk the uncomfortable, heady freedom by fighting back. Walked until each heel had a large blister and he was light-headed from the sun; then he'd caught a stage and used some of his seventeen dollars.

He'd arrived at his destination by asking the stage clerk for a passage. The man had looked at him oddly, then wrinkled his forehead.

"To where, pardner?" he'd said, mildly sarcastic. "You got to have a destination."

"Yeah." But Dexter hadn't known, so he'd reddened in spite of himself, and the clerk was staring at him more intently than ever, so he said what was in his mind, desperately, in a tight, breathless voice.

"You know of a place where there's trees, mister, and maybe a river or a big creek, and lots of open country — and grass, maybe?"

The clerk had smiled at him. "That sounds like heaven, stranger, not Arizona Territory." Then, having had his joke, the clerk had nodded at him, still with the close, wondering look. "I was raised in a place called Lovell. It's like that, sort of. Used to be a Injun fort. There's shade an' grass and a creek there. Dead little town, in a lot of ways, though."

So Dexter Williams had travelled to Lovell. Upon arrival he'd had thirteen dollars left, and his feet hurt like the devil because boots three years old didn't fit feet wider by inches. He felt more lost, forlorn, than ever, when he got down and saw the stores, the riders in from the ranches, the freight wagons and the open, frank faces of people who had never been to prison.

The second thing he'd done had been to apply to the stage company for a hostler's job. Dex was a horseman, not a cowman. That's what had landed him behind those big adobe walls in the first place.

But John Turnbull, the stage line founder's son, who was manager at the Lovell office, had turned him down after listening blank-eyed to Dexter's story. Then the third thing had happened to him. He had decided, rather desperately, to go up one side of Lovell's main roadway and down the other side, systematically, until he found a job. The astonishment, then, was complete when the first place he went was Herndon's Saddle Shop next to the Green Springs Stage and Transfer Company, told Herndon he wanted work, and got it. He thought back to that day, too. Six months ago, it had been. Herndon's liquid dark eyes had held him motionless; then he'd put aside his edging knife and pointed to a roll of evil-smelling, dark-looking leather.

"Know what that is?"

Dex had known. "Latigo. Smells like Mexican stuff." Will had looked back at him again. "You ever sew skirts and tugs?"

"Yes."

"I hate those jobs. What's your name?"

"Dexter Williams."

"Dex, you're hired."

The gratitude made his eyes sting. He remembered that. There'd been a solid feeling of guilt, too. "Mister Herndon, I just got out of prison."

The shock had shown in Will's handsome eyes, but a quick, embarrassed truculence came up to hide it in an instant. "Well, I reckon there's a lot of us that'd be there yet if we'd been caught at some of the things we've done in our lives." It was a quick passing over of a very awkward subject, and did Will Herndon credit. Also, it was one way to look at it. Then Will went on again, grappling valiantly to break the silence that was descending between them in the shop. "You don't have any hand tools, do you?"

"No. I never really worked in a harness shop before. Just around ranches and liverybarns, and places like that."

"Fine," Will lied grandly. "I never did like those saddle-makers who brought their own tools and sneered at mine. Well, Dex, first thing in the morning; all right?"

"Yes, Mister Herndon, and thanks."

The doe-brown eyes had snapped. "Will. Just plain Will. No thanks; I need a man bad. Look there; saddle-skirts half-way up the wall. Man, you'll never thank me again."

But Dex had, in his mind, anyway, and often, because that third thing that happened to him was the bridging of an abyss that he recognised as being the most dangerous one an ex-prisoner faces. Readjustment to society; finding an honest niche; getting his feet solidly under him.

The fourth thing was in his mind while he worked, listening for the sound of spurs that he half-hoped, half-feared, might mean customers coming in. So, when he heard the sound and looked up, Will Herndon's daughter was walking toward him with a high flush of something that may have been defiance, marring the smooth, cream-gold of her complexion, and the liquid dark eyes she inherited from her father were unflinching before his answering grey glance. She was the fourth thing.

"Margaret," he said matter-of-factly, a way of greeting he had that was more statement than hello.

"Dexter, I just heard." She went toward him, tall and strong looking; even-featured with ebony hair and wonderfully-arched eyebrows.

He watched her, feeling the same fullness she always inspired in him in spite of the fact neither of them had ever said anything that meant he was other than her father's employee, or she Will's daughter — his housekeeper in the widower's domicile.

"How *could* Tom Bulow think you did it!"

He almost smiled at the aghast defiance in her face. Instead, he leaned back, looking at her. "Pretty hard for him not to, Margaret. His reason's sound enough."

She knew he meant his prison background, but brushed it aside with an imperious toss of her head that was so regally like her. "That's not fair, Dexter. Not fair at all. Tom should know it better than any of us. He handles criminals every day, almost." A little of the resentment faded before his steady glance.

"And — well — you've been in Lovell six months. Doesn't he think, if you'd been going to do anything like that you'd of done it before?" He said nothing at all. Margaret's last shred of indignation wilted; then: "Dexter, what happened?" It had a leaden, muted sound to it.

"Someone knocked the guard over the head, pried open the safe and got away with nine thousand in cash. I was here, in the shop, when the guard said it happened. I didn't hear anything. That's what's bothering the sheriff. The guard said he hollered; maybe, but I didn't hear him."

"Oh," she said, "then Tom doesn't have anything to — to — associate you with the crime, then?"

"No; only that I'm who I am, Margaret."

She flicked her head a little, curtly. "And there's no one to say you didn't do it, but there's meanness enough in Lovell to think that you did."

"I can't prove I didn't, if that's what you mean."

"And he can't prove you did, either."

"No; but there's my record. He can use me until something better comes along — if it does."

"Oh no he can't," Margaret Herndon said quickly. "Who do they think they are?"

"The law," Dexter said flatly. "The law has a lot of rights you don't know about."

She looked down at the pile of work near the cutting tables as though fascinated by it. Some suspiciously illegal thoughts were running in her head, but her face didn't show it at all. She looked up again, suddenly. "Where's Dad?"

"The sheriff wanted to see him. He went up there."

"Thanks, Dexter. I'll go find him." She stood still looking at him; seeing the fear and helplessness in his face. "I'll — we'll — be back." There had been more, but she hadn't said it. He watched her go, then let his gaze wander over the subdued, shady somnolence of Lovell. A pinprick of hurt was behind his eyes.

Lovell was just a small cowtown. He had come to like it very much. It was far enough from the trails not to be wild, although occasionally a gunhawk would ride through; and he identified himself with the town, too. He belonged in Lovell. It wasn't just the desperate inner hunger to belong that made him feel that way; it was also the drowsiness, the unhurried bustle, the solidness of the place. Lovell wasn't a trail town. It was here to stay. A good place to put down roots and raise sons to carry your name . . . He was still sitting like that when Will came back.

"Was I right?"

"Dead right," Will said, tossing his black hat aside. "Right as rain. He wanted to know if you were reliable. If you worked nights very often, and so forth."

"Did you see Margaret?"

"Margaret?" Will said, as though his mind was having trouble coming back from urgent things to face less urgent ones. "No. Was she here?"

"Yes. Went up looking for you."

"No," Will said, "I didn't see her." He banished the irrelevant with a gesture, went over and dropped sideways onto a sewing-horse. "Dex, Tom Bulow always was a hard one to figure out. You can't say for sure whether he thinks you did it or not."

"Sure he does, Will. In his boots I'd think the same way."

"That's decent of you t'say so; but anyway, I'm not sure about him. He's always been a hard 'un to figure."

Dexter made a cigarette. "You know that skinny deputy he has? There's one that's sure I did it."

Will's brown eyes reflected contempt. "Slim. Slim Barr. No one takes him serious, Dex."

Margaret walked in. Both men turned and

glanced at her. She was wearing defiance like a badge, again. "They can't prove you did it, Dexter."

"Why?"

"Because I told Tom I was in the shop with you. Came down here and sat with you." The dark eyes shone triumphantly, but Margaret Herndon's face was flushed scarlet. "There," she added as an afterthought, "is proof you didn't do it."

Dexter wanted to groan, and her father did: a dolorous, soft sound. "Honey, why did you say that?"

"Because Dexter hasn't a witness that he was here all the time. Without one, Tom can lock him up whenever he gets ready — I think." She showed indecision and acute embarrassment for the first time. "Dad — ?"

"I understand, Marge," Will said. "Run along home and cook us a big supper, will you? I'll bring Dex with me an' we'll be hungrier'n wolves."

After she had gone, Will turned and looked at the saddle-skirt still clamped in his sewing-horse. But he did so with no intention at all of going back to work. He sighed and let his shoulders slump at the same time.

"Did you fall asleep, Dex?"

Shaken, not a little puzzled, Dexter was slow in answering. "You mean last night?

When I was working? No, I'm sure I didn't." Dexter put something into words that he'd been thinking about before, up in Bulow's office, but hadn't said. "You know how long it takes to sew a tug, Will. Well, I had two of them to do."

Will motioned with one hand. "I told Tom that. Told him that I couldn't see how you could've done everything the law thinks you did and complete two hand-sewn tugs as well. A man just couldn't do it."

"What did he say?"

"Nothing. Just sat there like an old owl, staring holes through me." Will arose, walked once around the office section of the shop, paused for a long, distasteful glance at the accumulated pile of paperwork on his desk-table, then went back and sat perched on the sewing-horse again.

Dexter watched him, felt ashamed and uncomfortable to be the cause of such anguish in the Herndon family, turned and went back to work. Sewing, he went over the thing right from the beginning, and all he was sure of was that guilt was firmly and not unjustifiably attached to him. In a place like Lovell, where everyone knew everyone else — and their business — a man like Dexter Williams stuck out like a red post on the prairie. Couldn't help but stand out.

He was still thinking like that late in the afternoon when Will called across the room to him, from the cutting-table where he'd been bending over a seating-leather pattern on a hide of stubbornly-upcurling leather.

"Let's go, Dex. Marge'll be wondering."

He looked up. There were mellow shadows outside. The day was gone. Surprised, he stared, and at that moment a man went by on the duckboards with an edging of white bandage showing from beneath his hat. It was John Turnbull, the first man in Lovell he'd asked for a job. Before he thought, Dexter stood up and crossed the room. Framed in the doorway, he saw Turnbull twist before entering the stage company's office and look back.

"Turnbull —" Walking toward the taller, less muscular man, Dexter wondered what he'd say. What he finally did say, was innocuous enough. "You get hurt?"

"Yeah, a little." The man's face was blank, matching his frosty eyes. "A little clip on the head is all." It sounded as dry as a late summer zephyr rustling old corn-stalks. Dexter understood in a flash.

"You were the guard — last night?"

Turnbull regarded him steadily, neither friendly nor unfriendly. "Yup, I was the guard."

28

"I didn't do it."

Turnbull's glance showed nothing, but the quick way he answered was an equivalent way of saying he didn't like the conversation. "I never told anyone you did, Williams."

Dexter felt foolish, standing there like that. Out of the corner of his eye he saw a man approaching them. He shifted a little and recognised the tall, lean deputy sheriff. "I just wanted to tell you, Turnbull," he said lamely, "that I had nothing to do with it."

The deputy came closer, ignored Dexter, and addressed himself to the taller man. "No trouble is there, John?"

"No trouble, Slim." Turnbull didn't look back at Dexter at all before he went on through the door and left the two of them standing there in hostile silence. Dexter could feel the antagonistic glance of the lawman. He refused to turn and look at it. Instead he went back the way he had come, met Will locking the door, then the two of them struck out for the Herndon home, and supper.

And it was good, too. A man could have all the trouble in the world on him, but so long as he had a stomach, he'd appreciate a meal like Margaret had gotten. The conversation was perfunctory. It ran in fits and starts until the coffee came; then the girl took things firmly in hand and steered them easily so that the evening was a success after all. Will arose and pushed fingers through his hair.

"How about a little three-handed black jack?"

Dexter was shocked, and showed it. Margaret laughed; the sound banished the last of the gloom. "Dad raised me like that, Dexter. I'm a sinner. We play cards almost every night."

Dexter considered the thing objectively, decided on the spur of the moment it must be all right, and smiled as he arose. "I'd like to very much," he said, "but I don't think I've ever played with women sitting in before."

"Then," Will said roughly, "you've never played at all, son. Come on."

They played for two solid hours, and Dexter lost ninety-one cents to Will's twenty-seven cents, and Margaret was the victor. So when she arose to get them some coffee, her smile was shades more dazzling than before. Will growled deep in his throat and berated women in general, his daughter in particular, then leaned far back, yawned, stretched, and reached across the table for Dexter's tobacco sack and papers.

"You thought what you'll do about this thing, Dex?"

"There isn't much to think about, Will. Either they'll lock me up or they won't. I can't do much about it."

Will lit up, inhaled and tossed the sack back across the table. "You know Marge was trying to help you to-day, don't you?"

"Yes, and I'm grateful, only —"

"Yeah; she lied. Well, Tom ought to be used to that by now. I don't suppose lawmen meet many people who don't lie to 'em for one reason or another."

Dexter shrugged. "I don't think that'll hurt me any, Will." He wasn't as sure as he tried to make it sound, though. The law might be lied to every day, but that didn't make it like liars or their friends any better.

"I can't see that Tom has much against you beyond his own darned suspicions though, Dex."

Dexter wanted to say that was enough, right there, but he didn't. Will wouldn't understand how the law worked toward previous offenders, and if Dexter told him, Will would blow up like he did infrequently. Then the beautiful, soft brown eyes would burn like rusty flame in the setting of his strong face. He was saved from having to say anything when Margaret came back with three mugs of coffee on a plank tray. The men waited until she'd finished serving them, then drank it black. Margaret used cream, but no sugar. She stirred the coffee and spoke without looking up.

"Doesn't it seem odd to both of you that there were no strangers in town before the robbery? I mean, don't men like that study over the place they're going to break into? Or do they just come in the night and know right where to go?"

Will smoked, saying nothing and staring into his coffee cup. Dexter eyed him askance and wondered, then said what he felt must have prompted the law's suspicion of him.

"That's it, Margaret. There weren't any strangers. No gunmen or hard-cases. Just Lovell's usual folks — and me."

She shot him a quick look from under long black lashes. "I'm sorry, Dex. I didn't think how it'd sound. I didn't mean —"

"He knows what you meant," Will growled without looking up from his coffee cup. "Don't be so touchy, you two."

Dexter eased the tension with no trouble at all. "I can't afford to be touchy. Not when I'm ninety-one cents poorer than I was."

Will chuckled, and Margaret's look of understanding was framed in a small smile. "Thank you," she said.

Dexter left after that. He walked through the stillness and saw the night as a prism of clearness that made the stars appear not more than ten feet away. He walked past the Con Brown Saloon, although his room was upstairs above the cardroom, and kept on walking until he was among the tarpaper shacks at the very edge of Lovell. Out there the range began and the duckboards petered out. He stepped down onto the worn ground and walked through the darkness until he came to a wind-twisted old tree, and there he dropped down on the grass, leaned back, and relaxed.

The sheriff would wait, Dexter knew that. He'd wait until he had something — just anything — that would point toward Dexter Williams or away from him, and in the meantime there would be days of this same agonising uncertainty. Maybe weeks of it, when he wouldn't want to look folks in the face, and maybe it'd hurt Will's business, too. Even if it didn't, it would hurt both Will and Margaret — he'd never had the nerve to call her Marge, like everyone else did — if not directly, at least obliquely.

Dexter was free. He thought about that, too. Marvelled at it. The other time he'd run afoul of the law it hadn't taken an hour for him to be locked up. Why was it different this time? Tom Bulow was as hard as granite, so it wasn't anything as squeamish as sentiment or doubt that kept him from putting Dexter away. He shook his head and made a cigarette.

The Herndons had come to his aid like cougars. It made him feel good, and pained as well. He'd always thought a man's kin would do that, but other people, like Will and Margaret, who weren't even remotely related to him . . . They had loyalty to spare: it was inherent in their kind.

And Margaret's defiant lie had been to protect him. She had deliberately thrown herself in front of Bulow's suspicions for the sake of a man she'd known a little over six months. He was warm inside, thinking about it.

So, in the final analysis, it was the Herndons as well as something within himself that made him go back to his room. But he wondered if he wasn't a fool to go back. He could get a horse easily enough, just as he could get a gun. For a man beyond the pale of the law, or at least barely hanging onto its fringes of respectability, the first way out of any trouble was to run. He considered it for a long time after he was in his room, sitting there in the darkness, smoking another cigarette, not wanting to light the lamp; finding solace and relief in the stygian blackness of the stuffy cubicle.

He could ride out of Lovell just as he'd come in, unnoticed. He could keep right on going until he was a thousand miles away. Up in Wyoming, for instance, where a man who knew as much about saddle and harness making as he'd learned could start all over again.

No. Someday something like this would happen again, and he'd have to run some more. It might even go on happening for the rest of his life, and he'd always have to run. The alternative was frightening. He'd stay; if Tom Bulow got him, and he went back to Territorial Prison again — that second time the warden had spoken of — then he'd go. But a man couldn't spend his life running, not when he wanted what Lovell had to offer as badly as he did. Wanted to belong as a cast-off puppy wants to belong.

He crossed the room, raised the sash and flipped the cigarette out in an end-over-end spiral down into the manure-stained roadway below. He stood breathing in the fragrance of cool night for a moment, then went back to the little table and felt in the darkness until he found the lamp mantle. He lifted it, struck a sulphur match that smoked and spluttered, laid it against the wick and re-set the mantle. The light clawed its way weakly around the wick, smoked a little because the wick hadn't been trimmed in a month; then caught and threw off a golden-range light that routed all but the corner shadows.

Dexter watched it for a moment, standing there so that his own shadow was huge and menacing on the back wall, then he turned slowly and gave a start.

Margaret stood up from the rocker, smiling self-consciously at him. "I'm sorry, Dexter. I didn't intend to frighten you."

He was a slow moment getting over his astonishment, then he leaned against the table, looking at her. "You're out late, Margaret."

"Yes." She moved toward him. "Dexter, you were gone a long time."

"I went for a walk."

"I imagined you would," she said. "There was a lot to think about."

"Yes."

She was looking up into his face. "There were horses at the livery barns, Dexter, and guns at the stores — weren't there?"

He didn't answer her. He didn't have to.

She reached out and touched his arm. "I'm glad you decided the way you did, Dexter." He could tell she was, from the way she spoke, the words coming in a relieved rush of breath past her lips. "And Dexter —" She leaned forward, took his chin in one small palm and brushed his mouth gently, furtively, with her lips, then let him go and went to the door before she finished it. "I didn't come here to check up on you, but to tell you that you aren't alone any more." Then she was gone, and he was standing against the little table with dumb shock in his eyes.

Chapter Two

He met Sheriff Bulow two days later. The lawman was standing stonily, watching Dexter
cross the roadway. Dex saw him from beneath
the brim of his hat, altered course a little and
walked toward Bulow in a straight line.

" 'Morning, Sheriff."

" 'Morning, Dex." He looked into the older
man's seamed, rugged face. There was nothing
there for a man to read, just the steady, unblinking impassivity. He took a short breath.
"Sheriff, when Marge told you she was there
at Will's shop with me —"

"She wasn't. I know." The slightly-stooped
shoulders rose and fell. "I didn't come down
in the last rain, Dex. You know why she did
that? To save your bacon. Women lie easier'n
men. You'll learn that if you live long
enough."

Dexter studied the blank face for a second
before he spoke. It was, as Will had said, impossible to figure Tom Bulow out. He spoke
as a man might who was repeating things he'd
said so often they were frayed and automatic
in his mind. No inflection at all. Statements

that were stripped bare of illusions and had only a little gravity left, the way the sheriff said them.

"Dex, if you'd heard some ruckus — a chair fall over, a grunt, some cussing, just anything — you'd of been off the hook with the law."

"No I wouldn't have," Dexter said. "I don't believe that. I'm an outcast here. You know that, and so do I. No matter what I said — if I'd been ten miles away — you'd of still thought of me right off, sheriff."

Another slow shrug that was eloquent of meaning, but no words.

Dexter tilted his hatbrim so the early sun wouldn't blind him. "Where do I stand?"

"Same place you did the morning after."

"No change until you get me, or clear me. That it?"

"Close enough, Dexter, close enough."

It was hard to control the sarcasm. "Thanks, sheriff."

He turned without seeing the tight, thoughtful nod, and headed back toward the saddle shop. There was more than the sick sense of hopelessness in Dexter. The shock was past. There was bitterness now as well. Bitterness and a growing sense of resentment.

He was just stepping up onto the duck-boards across the way when he heard the single pistol shot. His reaction, like the sheriff's and everyone else's who had heard the noise, was the same. Stop, look, and listen. There was no second shot. Will came out onto the plank-walk from the saddle shop and stopped under the overhang, squinting northward.

Dex went over by him and turned when he heard a distant shout. He saw the careening stage scattering dust and early-morning traffic as it came thunderously through town with the driver's boot kicking hard on the brake. The vehicle slewed in toward the duckboards before the Green Spring Stage and Transfer Company's office, and halted.

A big, dun-coloured cloud of pungent dust caught up with the stage and engulfed it, hung lazily in the air for a while, then fell back to earth. Dex and Will watched men erupt from the stage line's office and run toward the driver, who had leaped down and was standing beside the near door. The panel was open. Dex followed the driver's bent head and steady stare. There was a dead man dangling a little out of the opening. He was well dressed, what Dex could see of him, and his shirtfront was scarlet with blood.

Will spoke jarringly on the inhale. "Lord!"

Then the crowd closed in and cut off their view. Dex felt a heavy, ill sensation in the pit of his stomach. Will spoke again. "I was afraid that's what it was."

"What? The pistol shot?"

"Yeah. Signal to clear the road, the stage's coming in with trouble. Used to mean only runaways. Now it means anything."

Sheriff Bulow went by them calmly enough. Trailing some distance behind was his son, Eb, and the other deputy, Slim Bart They were hurrying and excited-looking. It struck Dex as dourly amusing. The man in the coach was dead. He had seen that from where he and Will were standing. Hurrying wouldn't help him; he was beyond needing help.

Then he saw the reddish, rusty hair of a lean, hawkish-looking man getting out of the stage, over the heads and hats of the men crowding in close. There had been another passenger, apparently, and this one was alive. The glance Dex had was a fleeting one. The man was quickly shunted into the stage line's office. Sheriff Bulow's old hat was bobbing in his wake.

Dex turned away, entered the shop and hung his hat on the buck-horn rack. Nice, quiet little out-of-the-way place, Lovell. He eyed the new hides of skirting leather with an acrimonious smile bare of mirth. Good place to put down roots, raise sons, live out the years. His bitterness returned, compounded; with it was wonder. What had caused this abrupt change in the place? His coming? Was he bad luck, too?

"Odd," Will Herndon said, strolling back into the shop. "Seems like nothing happens until, all at once, everything happens."

"Yeah," Dex said, "and it looks like the stage line's in the middle — along with me." He picked up a half-moon skiving knife and began to hone it absently. "Do they get robbed often?"

"The stage line? No. As far as I can recall it's been years since they've even had a horse go lame. The old man, Fred Turnbull, was a holy terror in the early days. Used to hang highwaymen with his own posses made up of company men. He inspired a whale of a lot of respect in outlaws." Will crossed his arms and leaned back on the cutting table, looking thoughtfully out into the sun-splashed roadway.

"When he started the line you had to be tough and merciless. He was both; any oldtimer'll tell you that. Then he got old, and young John took over. I've known John for twenty years and better. He never talked much, and still doesn't." Will shrugged and looked at Dexter. "John's been running the line for about two years now."

They went to work after Will's reminiscences died out. Lovell's small sounds came and went, unheeded. Each was busy with his

41

own thoughts until Tom Bulow walked in casually; then they both looked up.

"Got a job to do, Will," the sheriff said. His tone was quietly assertive.

"What?" Will straightened up, as Dexter did, too. There was something in the sheriff's bearing that aroused them both.

Bulow nodded slightly toward Dexter. "Ask a few questions. We can do it here or up at my place."

Dexter sensed peril. It was like a big fist closing around his heart, squeezing. "You want to talk to me, sheriff?"

"I do." A sidling glance at Will Herndon. "You mind, Will? I can take him to the office."

"Go ahead," Will said flatly. "Talk."

Bulow went over very deliberately and straddled a stitching-horse. He fixed his impassive, steady glance on Dexter. "The stage was held up north o' town a ways. At Latigo Grade, to be exact. The mail pouches and strongbox were taken." He saw an interruption coming from Will, whose face was darkening, and warded it off with a gesture of one hand. "Now let me finish, boys." He looked at Dexter again. "This here outlaw deliberately shot a passenger and killed him. Rode in close after he'd ordered the driver and the other passenger to the far side of the coach — and shot the feller with

42

his carbine, right through the window." Bulow paused to let it sink in, then he went on again.

"The driver never got a good look at the gunman, but the passenger did. He figures the other fellow was shot because he got a look, too, an' maybe even recognised the outlaw — or at least the renegade thought he'd seen him well enough to identify him. Well, that's guess work, but the main thing, Dex, is that holdup feller wasn't wearing a hip-gun. Held 'em up with a carbine."

The little weight of silence grew in the shop when Sheriff Bulow stopped speaking. Will's large, soft dark eyes were glued to Bulow's face and his lips were pulled in flat against his teeth. Dexter understood the sheriff's innuendo easily enough, and the feeling of futility lay in his stomach like a heavy weight. He wanted to swear at Bulow's calm, blank look; instead he asked a question.

"When did it happen?"

"About four this morning."

Dex swore then. The other time he'd been alone and had heard nothing. This time he had been asleep — again alone — so the finger of suspicion was pointing more damningly than ever.

"That'll do," Tom Bulow said, finally. Dex stopped swearing and glared. The silence was thickly oppressive. Will was leaning on the cutting table, both broad hands palms downward, fingers extended, as though bracing himself against a blow.

Dex let out a long breath, raggedly. There was nothing but despair in the air he breathed. "I'm it again."

Bulow's unwavering stare held to the younger man's face. "Well, where were you this morning, about four or thereabouts?"

"In bed, naturally."

Bulow nodded that time. "Sure," he said.

Will was regarding the sheriff steadily. "Tom, what're you stalling about?"

The sheriff almost grinned. It came very close. He answered without taking his eyes off Dex's face. "Reckon men get to know one another, don't they, Will?"

The saddle maker nodded very slowly. "They sure do."

Bulow raised a hand, held it aloft for a moment, then let it drop. The signal was obvious. Three men came into the shop from out front. Dex recognised them all. Eb Bulow, Slim Barr, and the red-headed stranger who had come in on the morning stage. He understood what Sheriff Bulow had been doing. Talking to him, holding his attention, while the deputies steered the survivor's attention to Dexter Williams.

The full significance of his situation was glaringly apparent. The highwayman had worn no belt-gun or shell-belt. He was a killer who had evidently shot down a man in cold blood because he feared detection. And Dexter Williams was already under suspicion for the previous robbery of the stage company. For the first time since he had come to Lovell, he knew fear in his heart. Solid, disheartening fear, the kind that was weakening, robbing a man of hope and wrenching the knowledge he had of his own absolute innocence out of him, leaving the cornered feeling of a desperate man in its stead.

When Bulow spoke, Dex's eyes went to the red-headed man. He was tall. His hawkishness of countenance was more pronounced, up close. Possibly in his late thirties, he had the look of a seasoned plainsman from the whipcord length of his sparse body to the direct, wary glance of his hazel-coloured eyes. He stood there in the fetid silence of the saddle shop, staring at Dex.

"That's him. Clothes an' all."

No one spoke for the space of a long clock tick; then Will Herndon's expelled breath came scratchily into the silence. "Tom, I don't believe it."

"No," the sheriff said, watching Dex like a hawk, "an' I don't reckon Margaret will, either. Dex, have you a gun on you?"

"No."

"All right. Hope you're not lyin'."

"I'm not."

Sheriff Bulow spoke out of the side of his mouth. "Eb, take him up to the office. Lock him up. Slim, take Mister Bauman back to Turnbull's office. I'll be along directly."

Dexter hadn't moved. His mind was in the grip of a sickening thralldom. The icy eyes of the warden at Territorial Prison jumped up out of recollection and were staring at him; then he had that feeling of trying to shout underwater again.

He hadn't committed either crime. He was as innocent as any man living, but that wasn't going to save him this time. Nothing was going to save him, unless it was Dexter Williams himself. He watched the younger Bulow come toward him; could tell by the deputy's face that his own was reflecting the tumult that raged within him. Turning his head a little, he could see the look on Will's face. It was a look of shock, more than anything else. Shock and indecision.

"Easy, Dexter," Eb Bulow said, stopping two feet in front of him. "Don't be a damned fool and make things harder for yourself than they are."

It was the sound of the man's voice that

made Dex relax. The futility of trying to prove himself — an ex-convict — innocent in the face of a living witness who accused him of a crime he knew nothing about left him aware of the dregs of bitterness. He slumped a little, reached up, took out his tobacco sack, and began to twist up a cigarette. Without seeing young Bulow's face, he could sense the deputy's relief.

Dex watched Bulow fish out his own tobacco. His glance went beyond, to where Will was watching them with terrible fascination, and beyond Will to the open door where Tom Bulow was going out behind Slim Barr and the red-headed man. He raised the cigarette to his lips to lick down the paper. He knew Will was watching them both; knew, too, that his own eyes showed what his face didn't show. The abrupt and raging inner ferocity that was within him. Something that had come out of the bitterness and the despair.

They were going to make an outlaw of him. He had no choice any longer. A yellow dog will fight for his life. He licked the cigarette, hung it in his mouth, reached into his pocket for a match with one hand, reached behind him with the other hand. He closed his fist around the razor-sharp skiving knife, felt its ash handle in his sweaty palm, then flicked the match, lit his cigarette and held the match out. Young Bulow leaned forward, took one draw, then became rigid, his eyes seeking Dexter's over the dying flame.

"Freeze!"

Eb did; in fact he hardly breathed. The skiving knife was an awful weapon. It was already through his shirt and pressing murderously into his stomach.

Dex's voice was as soft as nightfall, and as ominous. "Make a move, and everything you had for breakfast'll be on the floor." He dropped the match, reached gropingly for the deputy's hip-holstered gun, tugged it free and used the gunbarrel to replace the knife. Eb Bulow exhaled a little, and colour ran in under his bronzed cheeks.

"You're making the biggest mistake of your life, Dexter."

"No choice," Dexter said curtly. "You boys want an outlaw bad enough to make one. Turn around."

Eb was moving stiffly, unnaturally, when Dex's gun made a short, vicious arc. The deputy crumbled like a half-filled grain sack. Will Herndon's shoulders jerked with the blow. His large, handsome eyes were round.

"Dex!"

"Will, I didn't want it this way. Before God I had no hand in that robbery, any more'n

I had in the office holdup. What else could I do?"

"Nothing, I reckon," Will said mutedly. "But you've made it worse now."

"I couldn't have. They had me all lined up, Will. I don't know whether Bulow needs someone to crucify for these things or not, but I *do* know I'd stand about the same chance as a snowball in hell, in a Lovell court. You do, too."

Will looked deliberately at the unconscious man on the floor. "Hope you didn't crack his skull," he said.

Dex looked down, too. There was a stingy trickle of blood running through the deputy's hair. He shrugged, feeling no particular interest in the lawman. "Will — Marge . . . I don't know what to ask you to tell her." He lifted his glance to Will's face. "She won't understand this, will she?"

"I don't know."

"Well, I can't make her understand. Can't make anyone understand — or believe me, either, it looks like." He stepped over Bulow.

"Now what? What'll you do?"

"Get a horse and make tracks. I don't know where. Will? I'll come back someday; tell Marge that, will you?"

Will nodded, saying nothing.

Dexter stuck the heavy pistol into his waistband and walked out into the blazing sunlight. There he hesitated for the briefest part of a second, then crossed the roadway, threading his way in and out of the traffic, and went very methodically up to a loaded hitchrack. When he'd picked out an animal built for speed and stamina, he untied him, stepped aboard, reined out into the roadway, and lifted him into a trot, northward.

The sun beat down into Dexter's bunched-up, tensed muscles. It was relaxing for the flesh, but had no effect on the desperation and bleakness in his mind. He thought ironically of how easily the law could turn a man into an outlaw; make him fight back when he didn't want to.

He also thought of the red-headed stranger, remembered his terse words: "That's him. Clothes an' all." It brought a hard smile to his face. At four in the morning you could line up a hundred mounted men, give another man a fleeting glance at them all, and they'd look alike. Clothes? The men of the range wore levis almost exclusively. Their shirts and hats wouldn't show much but faded, indistinct colour in the gloom of pre-dawn. And the idea that he might have been the outlaw — at least was under suspicion of having already robbed the stage company once — was easily planted in the red-headed man's mind. A few words from Tom Bulow would have done that. Slim Barr, with his known animosity toward Dex, could, and probably would, sow the seeds in the stranger's mind. After that, identification would be easy. Maybe the man even believed it himself.

But the highwayman had worn no belt-gun. He thought of that. Mulled it over and wagged his head wonderingly over it. With the exceptions of preachers and a few others, no man went unarmed, and those few usually carried hideout, little belly-guns, somewhere in their clothing. But no outlaw with an ounce of instinct would even go about without a pistol, let alone hold up a stage without one gun at least buckled around his middle. That single idiosyncracy, more than almost anything else, was damning evidence against Dexter Williams.

He rode until the shadows were long, then it was hunger that drove him into a twinkling of little orange-yellow squares that were a town. He ate, had the horse grained, and turned in at a hotel of sorts. And after that first stop there were others, nearly always northward, because he was drifting along on the sub-consciousness that prompted him to follow a route he'd vaguely and previously considered safest.

When he'd left Lovell he'd had a little

money. When it was gone he rode into another town — one called Mesilla — and put up his horse in the evening dusk, went to a cafe and ate heartily; then walked alone through the gathering shadows looking for a saddle shop.

What he found was like a kick in the midriff by an Army mule. It was two dead white posters, one tacked directly above the other, with a hand-drawn picture of him looking out. He read the wording with mounting panic. Two thousand dollars reward offered by the Green Springs Stage and Transfer Company for Dexter Williams. Wanted by the authorities at Lovell, Arizona Territory, for robbery, murder, escape and horse theft.

Dex turned away, scanned the town from beneath his hatbrim, and was infinitely thankful for two things as he struck out for the livery barn. For the dusk, and the fact that most of Mesilla was home to supper.

He rode out of town with the pain in his eyes turned into hatred. Turnbull's company was advertising him a bandit and highwayman; he'd make their word good for them!

He rode down the night over his own backtrail. The plan in his mind wasn't especially clever. It wasn't even sound; but it *was* original. Lovell had forced him to the lawless trail. Logically then, to Dexter Williams anyway, Lovell should pay the price.

It took him five days to get back to the country he had started from, and he was still riding the same stolen horse. There was a certain sense of excitement in living like a wolf; no night-fires, never travelling except parallel to arterial roads and always keeping a retreat in sight; watching constantly, always on guard. It became second nature to him.

And it was this very wariness that aided his memory of schedules when he saw the Green Springs' stage rocketing through the pre-dawn toward Lovell. He sat like a forked buzzard, astride the big grulla horse, watching the coach and four coming through the gloom. Gently he eased the horse down from the slight eminence and rode obliquely, so as to intercept the stage at a point where the driver would be forced to haul in his horses because of ruts. He was waiting when the sounds of the vehicle came close.

The driver was an indistinct blur with the lines in his hands. The coach itself loomed large and dusty. Dex rode out, lifted the horse into a tight little lope, and swung in on the near side of the driver. He didn't say anything. He didn't have to. The driver's head swivelled. He stared down into the gun-barrel and automatically hauled up on the lines. The coach slowed and stopped. The driver's eyes were large and shiny. Dex motioned with the gun.

"Get down."

He kept the man between himself and the coach. "You in there — get out!"

The passengers were an old cowman and his wife, two sleepy, eye-rubbing riders, and a short, burly man who might have been a drummer or a businessman of some sort. Dex lined them up with motions. He had pulled his hat low so that only the glint of his eyes was visible.

"Driver, you got bullion aboard?"

"No. Just mail."

Dex shook his head. "No strongbox?"

The driver hesitated, barely, then said manfully: "No."

Dex was watching him closely. He nodded saturninely. "All right, then you can just shuck your britches and underdrawers and drive on in, bare."

The driver's mouth fell open. Dex could see the lean, tall old cowman's handle-bar moustache quiver. The driver swore mildly in obvious astonishment. He was going to speak, but Dex didn't let him.

"That or crawl up there and toss the strongbox out of the boot. Dealer's choice, feller. What'll it be?" He lowered the gun so that it pointed significantly at the man's midriff.

"The damned box," the driver said, and

turned to step up on the fore wheel without waiting to be told to. He grunted twice, then heaved it down. Dex didn't look down when he nodded.

"All right; you folks get back inside and keep your hands empty. Driver, move out!"

He watched the coach gather speed, and smiled gently; then he shot the hasp off the strongbox, took the heavy little sacks and went back to his horse. It had been so simple . . .

There was a monotonous sameness to each robbery as time went on, just as there was to the constant fear and wariness that came to be the larger part of his haunted existence. The Green Springs company doubled their reward. Dex retaliated by driving himself hard, riding night after night, without sleep, doubling his depredations. Several times he gleaned facts that showed how Lovell in general, the Green Springs company in particular, and the whole of Arizona Territory as well, were aroused over this savage, terrible scourge of outlawry that was confined to the Green Springs company and the Lovell locality.

It was after his eleventh holdup that he saw the posse combing the range. He watched from a knoll of man-high sage, thought he recognised old Tom Bulow but wasn't sure, and evaded the band with no especial hardship.

After that, his wariness increased. Like a spinner-wolf he rode in the night and slept during the days except when he struck at the Green Springs stages, and in time he became exactly what he had fought against becoming for so long. An outlaw in all things. A deadly man with a gun, which he developed into through sheer boredom and loneliness, by hours of practice in remote places. And a man who thought as all hunted things do; for ever balancing risk against safety and deciding only when the factor of safety was the greater.

The days went by and accumulated into weeks that quickly became months. Dex Williams was notorious. Perhaps, because of the success, he was also growing a little careless. Or maybe it was weariness. Possibly it was the nagging, never-completely still, small voice of conscience that told him he was terribly wrong. Altogether and completely wrong. But he kept up the solitary reign of terror against the Green Springs company until the day that all the nagging, the weariness and slight carelessness, almost got him killed.

He was striking at a line he'd only robbed twice before. It was in the flat, plains country where a horseman riding in daylight could be seen for miles. There was sage scattered, but not enough of it to shield a man on a horse; so he used dawn, his favourite time of the day, to race in beside the stage and pistol-cow the driver into hauling up. The driver made no move toward his belted gun, and tossed it over the side readily enough. Even co-operated to the extent of climbing down from his high seat before Dex told him, and opened the door to the coach. Dex almost smiled at the man's perfunctory acceptance of the robbery when he called to the passengers.

"Climb down."

They did. Two women, a young, thin man in rusty serge, and a wizened, dark-skinned old man bent with years and with hooded old eyes that had a tawny, fearless look as he appraised the highwayman.

"I got a gold watch," the old man said clearly, staring at Dex's face and ignoring the gun, "or'd you prefer plunderin' the ladies?"

Dex shook his head. "Neither. Just the strongbox, if there's one aboard."

"Well, there ain't," the old man said in his waspish way of speaking. "So you'd better take the watch."

Dex looked over at the driver. The man intercepted the look before Dex spoke, and shook his head by way of emphasis to his words. "He's right, Williams. There's no box."

"Business poor?" Dex asked dryly.

The driver shifted weight, shot a quick

glance at the old man, and said nothing.

"Yes; business is poor. Goddamned poor, Williams. Twenty years ago I'd a shot that gun out'n your hand. Now all I got left is my tongue, so it'll have to do."

Dexter looked at the old man, and a memory of something someone had told him long ago tried to come out of the vagary of his recollections. He squinted with the effort.

"Who're you?"

"Frederick J. Turnbull. That mean anything to you?"

Dex ignored the sarcasm. He studied the wispy, dehydrated frame and the ancient, ruddy old face. The founder of the Green Springs company. There was a grim measure of satisfaction in this meeting. "Yes," he said, "Will Herndon told me a little of you last spring."

The old man's eyes, watery but unwavering, bored into Dexter. "Tell me something, Williams. What's this all about?"

Dex smiled and jerked his head. "You want these people to stand here while we talk?"

"People be damned," Turnbull said bluntly. "My business is at stake. Let 'em stand or sit — I don't give a copper-coloured damn. That answer you?"

Dex nodded gravely. "It does me, yes. But I've a notion they don't care much about it."

He looked over at the driver. "Get it rolling," he said.

"Without the passengers?" The man looked incredulous. He, like the rest of the Green Springs campany's employees, knew Dex Williams' pattern of robbery so well any change was amazing.

"No," Dex said, motioning with the gun in his fist. "Put 'em inside and leave Turnbull here. Send a buggy back after him when you get to town."

The driver looked at the old man but was ignored in the steady stare Turnbull had fixed on Dex. "All right; get in, folks."

Dex watched the stage roll away, then turned slowly, holstered his gun and looked quizzically at Frederick Turnbull. "So your business is hurt, is it?"

"Hurt?" Turnbull said, and swore solid, old-fashioned, full-bodied oaths in his scratchy, quavering voice. "Why, damn you, I've lost two mail contracts. The one north out of Lovell to Gunnison and the —"

"I'm not interested, Mister Turnbull."

"You're not, eh?"

"No, I'm not. You asked what this is all about. I'll tell you." And he did. Turnbull listened stoically, weak old eyes seldom wandering from Dex's face. When he was through, Dex fished for his tobacco sack, twisted up a cigarette, and was suddenly conscious of the lightening of the sky and the incongruity of the two of them standing there, miles from anywhere, looking stonily at one another. Then Turnbull snorted. It was a short, explosive sound.

"Maybe it's like you say, Williams. Maybe you didn't rob the office or shoot down that passenger and rob us that second time, but you've sure played hell ever since."

"And you've raised the reward right along."

"My son did. I retired several years back. You've brought me back." Turnbull straightened up. He was thin to the point of emaciation. "In my day we'd of made short work of you, boy."

"Times have changed," Dex said through the tobacco smoke.

"Yeh, they sure have. Williams — I'll make you a proposition. You leave the company alone and give back what of the loot you've still got, and I'll drop all charges ag'in you."

Dex's smile was thin, unpleasant-looking. "How about Tom Bulow and his kind of law? Would he forgive me, too?"

"That's for him to say," Turnbull snapped.

Dex's smile widened, wolfishly. "No trade, Mister Turnbull. In the first place, Bulow'll haunt me until one of us dies. In the second place, I'm not the least bit worried about your company or what it'll do to me, and in the third place, I've got all but four hundred dollars of the money I've taken from Green Springs stages."

Turnbull's sharply indrawn breath was audible between them. "You've *what?* You mean to stand there and tell me you've got that money intact?"

"And hidden. Now, if you want to hire gunmen to hunt me down, hop to it — and you'll never see a cent of it."

Frederick Turnbull regarded Dex steadily through a long interval of silence, then he fisted both hands and jammed them into his coat pockets. There was a speculative, grudging grin on his face. "All right, Williams. It's your whip-hand. Deal 'em out."

Dex dropped the cigarette and carefully decapitated it with his spur rowel. "There's nothing to deal out. Green Springs company wanted an outlaw. They went out of their way to make one. I'm it. Well, take your medicine, Mister Turnbull."

"Goddammit," Turnbull swore, reddening. "I had no hand in what's happened. That —"

"Neither have I," Dex interrupted. "The Lord knows I did everything I could to stay within the law. The law didn't trust me, and your outfit sicked 'em on me. Well, *you* figure a way out; I'm content to go on like I am."

Turnbull brought one hand out of his coat pocket with a brittle smile. "Here. It's got your name on it."

Dex looked. The claw of a hand was holding a blue envelope in it. His heart lurched heavily within him, missed a beat, then caught up and went on as before. He made no move to take the note. He had never seen Marge's handwriting before, but instinctively he knew it then, on that azure paper.

"Well?"

"Take it back."

Turnbull held the thing out for a full minute, then slowly, reluctantly, let his arm drop. Dex's face was granite hard and expressionless. All but the eyes: there was anguish moving in their backgrounds.

"That was your ace-in-the-hole, wasn't it? Turnbull, your son should have your brains. You're quite a coyote, aren't you?"

Tumbull rocked back on his feet. He seemed to be considering something. Of a sudden he didn't look so old, either. There was colour in his parchment cheeks, high splotches of it under each eye. He withdrew his other fist, and Dex was looking into the under-and-over barrel of a .41 calibre Derringer. It was a murderously brutal little weapon at that range.

"No," Turnbull said in that scratchy voice, "her letter wasn't my ace-in-the-hole; this was. Dump that gun, Williams, we're going to start walking for town."

Dex stood motionless. He raised his eyes to the older man's face, then very slowly began to wag his head back and forth negatively. "Pull the trigger, Turnbull. That's the only way you'll take me in." Then he lunged. It was a desperate gamble based on his anger at himself for being deceived by old man Turnbull's ancient and decrepit appearance.

The explosion was thunderous and ear-splitting up close. Dex felt as though someone had struck him mightily in the chest. He had to gasp for breath. There was no sense of pain, just the shock and breathlessness; then he had the brittle wrist and forced it away from him easily. Turnbull made no attempt to grapple. He was staring wide-eyed at Dex, and breathing heavily. They were so close Dex could see the spasmodic, jerky contractions of the old man's nostrils, then he wrenched the little gun away, tossed it aside and stepped back.

That was when the stitch caught him in the side, made him fight back an instinctive desire to bend over. He went backwards a few steps instead, and sat down. Turnbull watched him. He looked up at him and made a wry face.

"Should've known better'n trust you, Turnbull. All right; you scored. Now head down that trail and keep walking."

Turnbull jutted his chin, Indian fashion, pointing. "Better plug that," he said dispassionately, "it's below your ribs from the looks of the blood."

Dex pulled out his pistol, laboriously cocked it, lifted it until it was centred on the old man's chest, then jerked his head sideways. "Walk, damn your old carcass, and keep walking."

Turnbull turned away abruptly and started down the ruts. Dex watched him for a while, then holstered his gun, opened his shirt and looked at the ragged hole just under his short-ribs. The bullet had penetrated his side and emerged out his back. The wound wasn't particularly serious, however, in spite of the bleeding.

He made a bandage-of-sorts of his shirt, then got up, and seeing the little hide-out gun lying nearby, went over and scooped it up. He went to his horse, got up by gritting his teeth, and struck out over the sun-blasted expanse of desert.

The pain didn't become acute until the constant jogging of his mount made it so, and by then Dex had seen the telltale dust-banners far south, which told him plainly that the Green Springs driver hadn't confined his information to the company alone. That was a posse, fanned out and riding hard. Dex cursed himself for bothering with old Turnbull, for now there was no place to hide, and escape lay only in flight, for long, gruelling hours with a flesh wound for company.

He rode steadily, and the thought that gnawed most at the edges of his mind where the spirals of pain didn't reach was the letter from Marge his bitterness hadn't allowed him to take.

She hadn't ever been out of his mind for long, during those savage months of outlawry, and Turnbull's offering of the blue envelope brought back, in a flood, all the poignancy that had haunted him for so long. He rode with Margaret Herndon's vision just ahead of him. As though the beautiful, dark eyes were encouraging him.

When he looked back the last time, bent over a little to ease the hurt in his side, the grulla horse was content to stand and breathe deeply for a moment's respite. The possemen were gathered in a dark knot, like ants, back where he had stopped the stage. The distance was too great to make out what they were doing, but three riders were coming over his trail, so he didn't tarry long, but slacked off his reins a little and let the grulla hit a long lope that was steady and mile-eating. He would shake the posse, he knew that, but he rode into the distances with one internal, and one external, hurt.

Chapter Three

Dex shook off the posse, but only because he persevered. Actually, it wasn't hard, with the lead he had, but the pain in his side was such that by the time he made it to cover, he was riding bent over and breathing in short, shallow gasps.

Recuperation was a slow process. It was six days later that he rode through the night toward Lovell. There was a fox-like shine to his eyes. His beard stubble was thick, and he'd lost weight so that it showed around the prominent cheekbones. He looked like what he was: a hunted man.

Lovell was steeped in shadow by the time he tied up and walked carefully through the back alleys to Will Herndon's place. Faintly, he could hear tinny music, and twice he heard loud yells of men; then he was in the shadows back by Will's horse-shed, blending, a lean-faced, staring silhouette of a man. There were lights in the house, and twice Dex saw Margaret's head, low over the sink. She was washing dishes, he surmised. He shifted weight, studied the house a moment longer, satisfied himself Will and his daughter were alone, then centred his attention on the surrounding houses and yards. There was nothing in the feel of the night that was peril. He eased away from the shed, went up to the back door, tossed a pebble against it, and stood back. Thinking ahead had become second nature.

Margaret opened the door and looked out. He was back in the shadows of an old apple tree, and could see the faint frown from where he stood.

"Blow out the kitchen lamp, Marge."

She started so suddenly it was visible, hesitated, then turned swiftly and went back into the room, leaving the door open. In a moment the back of the Herndon place was dark. Dex waited a long second, then he crossed the yard, slid into the house and closed the door very gently. In the gloom he sensed her presence.

"Dex."

"It's me, Marge."

He heard the swishing sounds of her dress coming closer. His eyes weren't adjusted to the deeper gloom of the room when she went up against him with startling boldness, reached up with both hands, pulled his head down and kissed him firmly, almost roughly, square on the mouth. There was a quick catch in her voice as she moved away from his reaching arms.

"No. Oh, Dex. Why did you wait so long? I've — we've — been frantic."

"Marge," he said slowly, then let it die and started over again. "Marge — that kiss — what did it mean?"

"Why do you ask?" She said it with a tinge of exasperation in her voice. He could picture the way she'd throw her head back when she said it. He'd seen her do that so many times.

"Well, women kiss because they're relieved, or something like that; and they kiss because they're in love."

He could make out her outline by the time she answered. Saw the tight little nod of her head go up and down. "Dexter, I've been in love with you for a long time."

He winced from the almost ponderous solemnity of the way she said it, but the thrill went through him just the same. "And I've been in love with you for —"

"I know it, Dex."

He stopped in mid-breath, considered that, then decided hastily that a woman would sense a thing like a man's love before the man would, almost. Just as he'd developed the ability to sense danger, lately. "Marge," he said softly, feeling the strange weakness in his stomach, and saying no more. Just her name. "Marge."

"Not now, Dex. Wait right there. I'll get Dad."

He waited, letting his eyes run over the room, seeing things he hadn't been able to see when he'd first come in out of the night. And yet not seeing things clearly, either, because of the bittersweet sensation behind his eyes that was acknowledgment of her love and his personal dilemma. Then Will Herndon came into the room and stood still just in front of his daughter, studying the dark shadow that was Dexter Williams. Without moving his head, he spoke aside to Marge.

"Honey, light the lamp."

Dex could see her hesitate and glance at him. He shrugged. "Go ahead, Marge. We'll chance it."

"No chance," Will said, moving toward the single large window over the sink. "I'll cover this."

The yellow light came swiftly because the wick was still hot. Dex looked at them both and saw the identical look of astonishment in their faces. He made a wry, self-conscious smile. "It's pretty hard to keep clean, sometimes."

Will opened his mouth, then checked himself and looked around for a diversion. He found it in the granite-ware coffeepot, crossed to the wood-range and poked up a fire under the thing.

Dex fingered his hatbrim unconsciously. Will was regarding him again.

"Been missing a little sleep, too, I reckon," Dex apologised.

"Yeah," Will said dryly.

"You've lost weight," Marge said. "Dexter, have you been hurt?"

"Well — once, yes, but I'm over it now. That's why I'm here to-night." He told them about Marge's letter, his shooting by Frederick Turnbull, and something else that was in the back of his mind. Something that had come to him one morning when he'd been lying in his blankets with the fever. Will listened without moving, but Marge poured them coffee in thick mugs and put it on the kitchen table. They sat down then, and Dex forgot his appearance as he talked.

". . . That's why I risked it to-night, Will. To sound you out on this."

Will looked into the ebony sheen of his coffee and said nothing. His large, dark eyes were sombre; then he sighed. "What made you think of it, Dex?"

Dex drank quickly. The coffee was hot. "I woke up one morning thinking about it. Look at it like this and you'll see what made me wonder. Tom Bulow said the guard yelled. The guard must have told him that, himself.

I wasn't more'n eight or ten feet from John Turnbull, the guard, when he yelled. That's what made Bulow think I was lying, Will. I didn't hear a single sound of any kind. That wall's not more'n four, five inches thick. Will, *if* young Turnbull had yelled, I'd of heard him, dog-gone it all. I know it, and you know."

Will nodded slowly. "Tom Bulow knows it, too. Yeah, I'm beginning to see what you're driving at."

"The fact that I didn't hear any yell — any sounds at all — and was that close, Will, means there wasn't any noise. In other words, John Turnbull could've opened the safe himself — he had to, in fact, and he had to do it by the combination. If he'd used a crowbar I'd of heard that racket, too. I didn't hear a sound because there wasn't any noise made. Turnbull did it. Turnbull knew I was an ex-convict because he was the first man in Lovell I told about it, when I hit him up for a job. He robbed his father's company and used me as the victim."

Will drank his coffee thoughtfully. Marge was looking at Dexter with a tense, worried expression. The silence drew out into a long, thick covering in the kitchen; then Will Herndon leaned back in his chair and pushed the empty coffee cup away from him. "Dex, I've been piecing things together ever since it happened. Nothing fitted. This does, boy, but for the life of me I can't see *why* John would do it."

Marge made an impatient gesture with her head. "That's not the point, Dad. What matters is that he did it; worked it so carefully that Dex —"

Will smiled shrewdly, then laughed. It was a soft, quiet little laugh with a world of understanding in it. Then his face sobered again, but the glance stayed steadily on his daughter. After an interval, he sighed again and shifted on the chair. "Honey," he said, "if I was prosecuting Dex I wouldn't want you on the jury."

Dex's palms were slick and oily feeling. He had that peculiar sense of guilt and deception that goes with young love. Turning his head, he could see the give-away red colour in Marge's face and the look of stardust in her beautiful eyes. It made him feel all the more uncomfortable. Will would know now, if he hadn't suspected before.

"Two things I wonder about, Will."

Herndon looked away from his daughter. His glance seemed to drag as it lifted to Dex's face. There was a deep stillness to it, a very serious, unhappy sort of fixation. Dex saw the strange glance and wondered about it.

"I'm like you," Dex went on. "It seems so strange that he'd rob his own company that

I had to talk it over with someone — with you. It doesn't make sense to me, but I'll be damned if the rest of it doesn't fit perfectly with what I know about that first robbery."

"The other thing?" Will asked quietly, still wearing that solemn, pained look.

"The red-headed passenger on the stage, after the second robbery. He identified me right off." Dex shrugged. "At the time I figured he did it because I was handy and already under suspicion; later I got to wondering if maybe he wasn't put up to identifying me."

"By John Turnbull?" Marge said it, but it was more of a statement than a question.

Dex nodded. "Yeah, by young Turnbull."

Will was frowning a little. "What makes you think that, boy?"

"Well, why'd the outlaw just kill one of the passengers? Why'd he leave one alive, if he was trying to do away with folks who might be able to recognise him? That's one thing, Will. Another is the fact that the outlaw *wanted* to be recognised. It fits in with my idea about John Turnbull. Whoever held up that coach, Will, went out of their way to dress just like me. Even used a carbine to give the impression he didn't own a pistol. You know an ex-convict isn't allowed to."

"Why the dead passenger, Dex?" Will was watching the younger man intently.

"I don't know. My reason for that killing is weak. All I can say is that it'd make it certain that I'd be picked up, tried, and more'n likely hung, right away." Dex frowned into his coffee cup. "It seems like a hell of a reason to gun down a man, Will, I know, but Turnbull's playing a pretty hard game." He looked swiftly at Will's face. "That was something I wanted to ask you. Do you think he'd do a thing like that?"

Will's glance drifted away, caught on the covered window, and held there for a moment, then came back to Dexter's haggard face. "I think he's capable of doing a thing like that, Dex. I've known John a long time. Yes; I think he'd go that far to crucify a man — if he was going all-out to get him, anyway." He glanced unseeingly at Marge. "But why? What in the devil would make him rob his own company? John's got money; ought to have, anyway. Old Fred's well off."

"That doesn't mean John is, Dad," Marge said.

"Noooo," Will drawled softly, "but Fred'd haul John out of any scrapes he'd gotten himself into, rather than have the business hurt, I'd imagine."

"Sure he would," Dex said, "providing he knew about them, Will. Providing John'd tell the old man, but I can tell you from experience that the old man doesn't suspect anyone on earth of robbing his company but me."

Will shook his head. "Beats me, Dex; sure beats the hell out of me," he said. He held the silence for a while, looking moodily from one to the other of them. "And yet it fits pretty well, the way you've got it matched up."

Marge looked appealingly at Dex. "But, honey, you're still an outlaw," she said pointedly. Will's glance swung to her in a flash, stayed rivetted to her face while Dex answered with his crooked smile.

"I know, Marge. I went off half-cocked. I know it now, but right then — right when Bulow and the bunch of them were trying to nail my hide to the wall for things I didn't do — I didn't care. Like I told old man Turnbull; they wanted to make me an outlaw — all right, I'd oblige 'em. I'd be an outlaw and they'd pay my way."

She leaned her face in her hands. Her liquid dark eyes were enormous in the creamy setting of robust beauty. "You shouldn't have, Dex."

He made a helpless motion with one hand. "I know it, now, Marge, but it's done. There's one thing, though — I've got all but a few hundred of what I've taken from their coaches."

Will's glance flicked away from his daughter's face in a quick flash of astonishment. "You have?" he asked.

"Yeah. I'm short about five hundred, Will. Used that to buy grub with; but the rest of it's in the same boxes I took it in."

Marge's glance never left Dexter's face. "Give it back, Dex."

He nodded at her. "All right. Any time they want it, they can have it." What he said didn't sound incongruous to him at all. He hadn't ever robbed for the money, anyway. Will made a dry whistle and held his mouth puckered up afterward, regarding Dex with new interest.

"Listen, Dex, I've got an idea. I'll get Fred Turnbull and Tom Bulow together an' make them the proposition. You'll turn back the loot for a clean pardon."

Dex smiled wryly. "Will, they won't do it. Not either one of them. Bulow's after my hide, and old Turnbull wouldn't compromise with the devil for his soul."

"I wouldn't bet on that, Dex," Will said. "Bulow'd be hard to deal with, I know, but old man Turnbull's been hurt plenty by your one-man war against his company. Not just in prestige, but in cash and contracts, and that's what counts with him. I'll lay you odds he'll settle for the return."

Dex shook his head and smiled a little. "Maybe you're right, Will, but I've got something in the back of my head I want to try first."

"What?" Marge asked quickly.

He looked at her. "Well, if it's John Turnbull like we — like I — think it is, who's caused me all this grief, I want to know it. Also, I want the world to know it, and especially I want his father to know it, because the old man'd never believe anything unless he saw it with his own eyes."

"Agreed," Will said, impatiently. "What's in your craw, son?"

"Will, I want you to do me a favour."

"Sure; name it."

Dex's smile was almost apologetic. "I hid a pouch of new gold behind the first manger in your horse-shed. I want you to take it into the stage company office and ship it to Mesilla to the stage office to hold against you going there to pick it up." Will and Marge both look puzzled. Dex leaned back in his chair. The room was warm; it made the tenseness go out of him.

"I want you to be sure and get John Turnbull to accept and sign for the shipment, Will. There's six thousand dollars of the gold I took from the company in that pouch."

Marge's eyes were shining. "If John's the outlaw, he'll have reason to waylay the coach again."

Will's smile was thin. "Six thousand of their own gold. I like that, Dex, damned if I don't."

"Will you do it?"

"Sure; be glad to. When you want it to go out?"

"Take it in to Turnbull to-morrow morning. That'll put it aboard either the noon stage out or, if he misses that one, the evening stage."

"And you'll be handy both times? That it, Dex?"

"Right."

Marge's glance clouded over. "But, honey, you shouldn't try it alone."

"I'm not going to," Dex said. "I'm not even going to show up." At her look of bewilderment, Dexter leaned over the table. "Marge, if you and your Dad hint around that I'm going to hit the stages carrying the money — even to the point of asking Tom Bulow to do you the personal favour of riding with that six thousand — he'll do it. He's your friend; he'll do it all right, if for no other reason than to get a crack at me. Well, I won't be there until *after* he's got the highwayman, honey. That way there'll be no question about me being involved at all. I'll sort of hang back and follow both stages in case the highwayman gets away. Kind of a

78

rearguard for Bulow, y'see?"

Will Herndon slapped the tabletop gently. His large, brown eyes were snapping. "Dex, dammit all, you've got it. Why not have old Fred Turnbull ride the coach, too? He'd be right there when —"

"I don't know, Will. I'm afraid of that. He might tell his son what was up. If he did, there wouldn't be any robbery."

Will didn't give up that easily, though. He looked temporarily crestfallen, then straightened up again. "I'll get him aboard, boy, and he won't have a chance to talk to young John beforehand, either."

"How?" Dex asked, beginning to worry.

"Easy," Will said. "I'll get him down at the edge of town with me, walking, then I'll flag down the stage and boost him aboard."

Dex was frowning. He didn't like it, and yet he wanted Turnbull senior to be on hand, too. Finally he gave a slight nod of his head. "All right, Will, but if —"

"Don't worry about that," Will interrupted. "I understand."

Marge was looking at Dex with a little squint of worry. She didn't say anything, although she had opened her mouth to speak, because at that moment a heavy drumroll of knuckles across the distant front door thundered throughout the house. Dex was on his feet in a flash, all the panther instincts awakened. Will came up more slowly and Marge reacted with only her eyes. They were large and glassy with fear.

Dex spoke without looking at either of them. "You expecting anyone, Will?"

"No."

"Who's that knock belong to?"

"I don't know."

Dex nodded. "Answer it."

Marge got up then, the fear staining her face like acid. "What'll you do, Dex?"

"Nothing, honey. If it's trouble, they'll have the rear of the place covered, too. If it isn't trouble, Will'll come back and tell us."

Will moved lightly, on the balls of his feet. He crossed the room, passed beyond their sight, and the muffled echoes of his tread came back to them. Marge moved then. She picked up the third coffee cup and pushed it into a cupboard, saw an old, dirty deck of playing cards and on a wild, irrational impulse, took them back to the table, tossed them on it and looked up at Dex's strained, pallid face with its cold eyes. She plucked at his sleeve.

"Dex, go down there. The root-cellar, honey. Go down there and don't make a sound, and — and — take your hat," she said breathlessly, the pulse at the base of her neck beating raggedly.

He moved only after he heard the muted sound of men's voices. "Is there a way out, down there, Marge?"

"There's a little transom window, Dex, but it's too narrow. Hurry, Dex!"

But he'd heard the approaching pair of footsteps, too, and moved quickly to the little cellar door, opened it and groped his way down the earthen steps to the dank obsidian blackness below, where a musty, close odour enfolded him.

Standing in the stygian gloom, he could hear the shuffling bootsteps halt in the kitchen. The voices were indistinct until he strained to hear them; then his heart contracted within him. The third voice was unmistakably that of Sheriff Tom Bulow. He felt his way very carefully amid the shelves of bottled preserves until he was directly under the kitchen; then he leaned a little in concentration and nearly held his breath as he made out the muted conversation overhead.

"Will, the Turnbulls've been keeping men watching your place for a long time." Dex could almost see the steady, unblinking gaze of the lawman, and his impassive, smooth face. "They sent word that you'd covered the kitchen window." Bulow let his voice trail off. Dex understood the long silence before Marge spoke.

"Is that against the law, Tom?"

"No," Bulow said, "but it's sort of unusual, isn't it, Marge?"

Dex could picture her, too. She'd toss her head with that regally defiant way she had when she answered him. "Maybe, but we do things like that, Tom, when we feel like it. If it's caused Turnbull's spies some trouble, I'm not especially sorry."

"All right." Dex thought Bulow's voice sounded weary; tired to the point of indifference. "I won't ask you why you did it, Marge."

Will spoke. His voice had that sharp edge to it that Dex recognised. "We were playing cards, Tom. Just felt like a nickel's worth of privacy is all."

Dex smiled crookedly at Will Herndon's lie, and knew the older man had taken the cue from the cards Marge had thrown on the table.

"Sure," Bulow said dispassionately. "Will you answer me a question, Will?"

"Maybe, Tom. Maybe not."

Dex didn't wait to hear any more. He began a slow, very cautious search for the little window, and when he found it he let the breath go out between his teeth in a slow hiss. As Marge had said, it was a transom, and very narrow. He explored it for the hasp, found the thing, and worried it free, cursing inwardly at every tiny sound. Prying the warped frame away from its sill took more patience than time, but when the cool night air hit his face he leaned on the wall and breathed deeply.

The muffled voices overhead were running like swift water through a weed-choked creekbed when Dex fought his head and shoulders through the opening and drew in his stomach as much as he could in order to gain clearance for his midriff, with its laden shell-belt and pistol holster. The anxiety within him was greatest just before he pulled free and lay prone in a cluttered geranium bed, because he heard the people overhead moving.

Tom Bulow wouldn't force the Herndons to show him the house. He was too wise for that. But he could manœuvre them into the position of volunteering, simply by veiled implications that they were hiding the outlaw, Dexter Williams. Lying there in the crisp, cold air, Dex tried to figure which way Will and Marge were taking him, and hoped it wasn't the root-cellar they were going to look into first. He caught the lumpy, hunched-over outline of a squatting man with a stubby carbine that reflected the weak, watery moonlight, over by the horse-shed.

Bulow, or Turnbull, or someone, had laid a careful trap just in case . . . He lay flat, studying the man and knowing there would be others. He smiled to himself; but for his moment's rest he would have made a run for it. Sky-lining the yard showed no other men. He licked his lips and narrowed his eyes, then began a laborious crawl along the edge of the house, through the geranium-bed, until he was close to an old, rickety fence of split rails that divided the Herndon property from the adjoining place. There he studied the fifty-foot clearing he'd have to cross before he could again lose himself in the weeds along the rail fence.

The sentinel back by the horse-shed could see a man that distance, all right, but only providing he happened to be watching for movement. Dex waited until the guard had swung his head in the slow, careful arc he used for watching the yard, then he sprinted. No shot came. He vaulted the fence and threw himself flat, listening to the irregular thunder in his chest. It was the only sound. He felt immeasurably safer, and got to his hands and knees and began to crawl swiftly toward the alleyway.

Again luck favoured him. He made it without a sound; lay flat studying the galaxy of shadows that hung close to the littered little roadway, then pushed himself erect and merged into them, walking fast and slightly bent, as tense as a coiled spring, all the way back where he had left the horse. Then he got the most solid jar of all. The horse was still there, head down and drowsy, and there was also the unmistakable, dull glitter of moonlight off a rifle barrel behind a tree nearby.

Dex stopped, blending into the night, and knew that the horse had been discovered and identified as the one he'd stolen previously, and was being used as a baited trap for him. Death wasn't far from him. He leaned back against an old fence with damp, cool morning-glory vines thick and snarled on it, and bit back the fear that was rising up within him.

He stood like that for a scant few minutes, then turned on his heel and headed back through the maze of little paths and alleys until he emerged far south of Lovell's main thoroughfare. Once again he covered himself with shadows whenever he could, and studied the hitchracks where saddled horses of night revellers stood hip-shot and patient.

But the trapped feeling grew as he studied the town. Bulow's — or Turnbull's — trap was well set. Grimly and securely set for Dexter Williams. It was clear to the wolf-eyed man with the beard-stubbled face and fox-fire eyes. To an average person the casual, indifferent men who leaned or sat, watching each hitchrack, might have gone unobserved or have lacked significance. Not to Dex, they didn't. Death was waiting for him in Lovell. It was watching saddled horses, including his own, with slitted, deadly eyes. He stood there in the deep gloom, with fear thick under his heart for the first time since he'd turned outlaw, for the men arrayed against him were playing a wily game all their own, and they weren't fools by any means.

He made a cigarette and turned away over his cupped hands when he lit it. The smoke went deep into his lungs and came out in an eddying, tortured streamer from his nose. There were other horses in Lovell; that wasn't the point, right now. The point was that, whoever had laid this elaborate and clever trap, had also done a thorough job. He knew in his bitterness that each livery barn, each corral and stage-horse shed would also have a gunman waiting.

He visualised Tom Bulow's face with its impassive steeliness; its hard blue-eyed doggedness, and wondered if he were capable of working out a thing like this in advance, and so thoroughly. Bulow was capable of it all right, but somehow it just didn't strike him as the kind of thing the sheriff would take pride in. He might do it, but Dex thought it more likely that Tom Bulow, and even his son Eb, would go at a thing more directly, more bluntly and dogmatically.

He smoked, watching the few strollers out of the corner of his eye, and swore to himself. John Turnbull not only would have been able to think up such a careful plan, but would do it exactly as it had been done. He shook his head and dropped the cigarette, looked down and stomped it underfoot. A stark kind of antagonism swept over him.

So far Dex Williams had been forced to take all the chances and incur all the animosity. John Turnbull had done nothing but remain in the background, pull the strings. Dex's anger grew. It was more resentment than anything else. Turnbull had out-smarted him right down the line, and it had taken this immediate peril and the sense of helplessness — fear — to make him see it.

He studied the man across the roadway from him with a new flat look of challenge in his face. Considered the lanky, slouched frame for a long thoughtful moment, then shoved off the wall of the building he'd been leaning against and walked deliberately south, away from town, down toward the shoddy, tar-paper shack area where the 'breeds and drifters, and down-at-the-heel riders, lived their hand-to-mouth existence. Even made himself walk with the shuffling, derelict-gait of those denizens until he thought it was safe to cross the road.

Then he disappeared into the trash-littered lots that separated the shacks, turned northward once more and went stalking through the darkness back uptown.

When Dex emerged onto the plankwalk again, he was two buildings south of the long-legged frame of the guard who was watching the hitchrail he'd decided to steal a horse from. Drawing a deep, tremulous breath, he sauntered down toward the man, head down and feigning a slight limp. Close enough, he eased down onto the bench beside the man and raked one fast glance over him. Recognition was mutual, but Dex's handgun was in his lap; Deputy Slim Barr's was holstered, although his palm was resting on the walnut butt of the weapon. Barr's eyes shot wide open.

"Hold it, lawman. Just like you are."

Barr didn't move. When his astonishment passed, the same old antagonism was there in his unpleasant stare. Dex remembered it.

"Stand up and walk ahead of me, around the blacksmith's shop and out into the alley behind, but don't make a mistake, deputy. Don't make a mistake!"

Barr didn't. He moved a trifle stiffly, but he obeyed. Out back, Dex took his pistol and threw it away; then regarded the thin, dour-faced man thoughtfully. "Tell me something. Who thought up this surround?"

Barr shrugged. The wrath was shimmering in the background of his stare. "What's the difference?"

Dex cocked his head a little. "You're forgettin' you're not behind the gun this time, feller."

"No, I'm not," Barr said, "and I'm not for-getting who is, either."

"Then you make straight answers," Dex said, "unless you want the waddin' kicked out of you."

Slim Barr considered that for a moment. He had no illusions about who would win in a hand-to-hand scrap, either. For all his height, Williams was a powerfully put-together man; solid, as a granite boulder is solid, and hard. He shrugged. "Tom Bulow, as far as I know," he said.

Dex shook his head. "I don't believe that."

"Who else?" the deputy sheriff asked, with-out much enthusiasm.

"It doesn't matter." Dex eased down the dog of his gun. "Now listen to me, lawman, because I'm only going to say this once."

Barr began to shake his head. "It won't work, whatever it is."

"No? Why not?"

Barr's thin, hatchet features split in a stingy, mirthless grin. "Listen, Williams; we've been expecting you to come a-visitin' for a long time. We've made plans."

"Yeah, so I've seen."

Barr's grin persisted. "Not just guardin' the horse racks, either. Both ends of town are sealed off. Got men standin' at both places, north and south, day and night. You got about as much chance of gettin' out of Lovell as a snowball in hell."

"Both ends of the road're guarded, eh?"

Barr nodded curtly. "An' every damned corral in town's bein' watched, too." He shifted his weight, stood hip-shot and relaxed. "Best thing for you to do, Williams, is hand me that gun. Leastways you'll live out the night, that way."

Dex used a sardonic smile of his own. "Thanks," he said dryly, "but I don't like the Lovell brand of law."

"It's just as good as any other kind."

"Or bad," Dex said. "It's all the same. If you can't find an outlaw, make one."

Barr snorted. "Oh, hell," he said, "why don't you rope that stuff about bein' so innocent? Your actions lately've convinced half the country you were guilty right along."

Dex wagged the gunbarrel. "No future in arguing it with you, Barr. Right from the first you've had your mind made up I was guilty. Well, I wasn't; not then, but it doesn't make any difference now." Dex saw the reply coming and cut it off with a vicious oath. "Shut up; that's better. Now listen to me. Like I said, I'm only going to tell you this once."

The deputy reddened and his eyes flashed, but he held his silence.

"Walk across the road out there, to that hitchrail you were watching, pick out two good horses, untie 'em and bring 'em back here. Two horses, d'you understand?"

Barr's face was a study in astonishment and other things. He pulled his mouth flat. "You damned fool, you'll get killed."

Dex smiled thinly. "You will, too. Remember what I said? *Two* horses, lawman."

That time it sank home. Barr blinked his eyes rapidly, and a little of the ruddiness left his face. "You're takin' me with you? Why?"

"I'll tell you later. Now go fetch the horses, and remember I'm back here in the shadows. Fault me, feller, and you'll beat me to hell by half-an-hour."

The deputy sheriff didn't move. His expression was one of near panic. "I can't do it — dassen't try it, Williams."

"Why?" Dex sensed the urgency in the deputy's voice.

"Because — well — because there's another

guard in the store across the road. He'll know what I'm doing. Tom's orders are that no one's to touch those horses, no matter what."

Dex made a low whistle. The full extent of the trap to catch him was amazing. His forehead wrinkled and the eyebrows drew in over the high bridge of his nose. "Tom Bulow didn't think of all this, Barr." The deputy shrugged. "Who did? Spit it out, feller."

Barr's uneasiness was increasing. Slowly but surely it was being borne in upon him that he, not Dex Williams, was in the most dangerous spot. "Damned if I know. Tom give us orders, that's all I can tell you."

"All right," Dex said, "who's across the road, inside the store?"

"Feller name o' Clampett. He's a hostler at Morton's livery barn."

"Go over there and fetch back two horses, anyway."

"Williams —" the deputy began, his voice off-key.

"Never mind. You do as I tell you. If this Clampett gets rough with you, I'll take care of him, don't worry about that; but Barr, if there's shooting, you bring those horses back here on the run, or you and Clampett both'll be magpie bait."

Barr's desperation was acute. Suspicious and slow-witted by nature, he nevertheless had a full measure of fear in him. Dex saw the protest coming and stepped in close to the man, snatched a fist full of shirtfront, and shook him like a terrier shaking a snake. "Get going, damn you!"

Barr went, on legs that moved as though the joints were granite and the sinews were weak springs. Dex watched his back until the darkness threatened to engulf his man, then he moved cautiously down between the buildings, his naked hand-gun cocked and riding in his fist with lethal arrogance.

Barr crossed the road, went to the pair of saddled horses at the south end of the rack. He hesitated, half-looked back, then ducked his head like a man jumping into ice-water, and began unlooping the reins. He had both animals free, and was turning away when Dex saw the darkened mercantile store's doorway open a slit. Moving fast, Dex crossed the roadway, stepped up on the plank-walk and came down behind the thickly-made, very bow-legged men who was approaching Slim Barr with one hand on his belt-gun and a black scowl on his heavy features.

Barr stood helpless, seeing Dexter behind the man. An instinct, or perhaps the ring of a spur rowell, made Clampett turn. He hadn't completed the movement when Dex's gun swung in a tight, vicious overhand slash that ended abruptly against the other guard's cranium. The thick body went over head first like a toppled tree.

Dex didn't stop his stride, but stepped over the man, tore a set of reins from Barr's fist, and swung into the saddle with a violent oath and an order for the deputy to do likewise.

Astride, Dex jerked his head sideways. "Out through those buildings. Hurry up, dammit. Head out west of town across the range and hold steady west. Lope out, man!"

They rode in a mile-eating lope, neither saying a word. Dex twisted in the saddle once, and looked back. He thought he had heard a distant shout, but no recurrence came down the night to him to affirm the suspicion. He swung forward in the saddle and shot a glance at his prisoner, then settled down to the steady rhythm of his new mount.

Miles away from Lovell, Barr reined his horse down into a fast walk. Dex followed the lawman's lead, and in the stillness around them nothing but clumps of intermittent sage and the occasional gauntness of a tree broke the darkness. Barr turned to face his captor.

"All right, Williams. Why?"

Dex's teeth flashed in his smile. "Needed company is all. Just in case — you'll be my ace-in-the-hole."

"Won't do you any good," Barr said,

glumly. "Tom'll track you come daylight."

"Maybe. By daylight, man, we'll be so far from Lovell he'll need more'n trackers to find us."

And they were. Dex made for the fir forest where he knew the needles would hide their hoofprints. Back to his hidden camp where he'd nursed himself through Frederick Turnbull's shot. By the time they had made the fringe of trees and pushed on to the hidden meadow where the camp was, and swung down, Slim Barr was grey with weariness. He stepped down like a man with bones of glass; gingerly, with no give to him at all.

"Now what, Williams?"

Dex looked across the seat of his saddle at him. "What's so all-fired important, Barr, that you've got to keep asking questions?"

"Nothing," the lawman flared up, "nothing at all. Why the hell would a man have any interest in what's going on when his life's likely to be in danger — and he hasn't got a chance to fish or cut bait?"

Dex relaxed a little. "Well, forget it. You're safe enough now and can catch a little sleep. We'll be riding again in another couple hours. Until then you haven't got a worry in the world."

"No," Barr said heavily, "not a worry in the world. Just disarmed and a prisoner of an outlaw is all. Nothin' much in that to worry about, is there?"

Dex bent, hobbled his horse with the circlets off the saddle, then unsaddled, slipped the bridle and watched the animal crow-hop away. It wasn't a bad animal, at that, considering the night had been dark and —. He turned toward Barr.

"How long you been guarding those horses?"

"The last four nights. Before that . . . Oh, you mean the animal?" Barr shook his head. "We just used whatever critters the riders rode in from the ranches. Didn't let folks know what was going on in case some of 'em might be friends of yours."

Dex smiled. "Well, you made a good pick to-night, Barr. Should have been a horse thief." The deputy began to unsaddle. He said something, but it was indistinct, and Dex didn't press for a repetition. "You boys kept it away from the Herndons especially — that right?"

"Of course. What'd you take us for?"

Dex's grin widened. He felt good after eluding the trap set for him. "Might hurt your feelings if I told you."

Barr shot him a venomous look, then dumped his saddle and bridle and ignored the horse that minced away from him in hobbles.

"Where was you to-night?"

"At the Herndon's."

Barr didn't move for a moment, then he nodded his head ever so slightly. "Just like I figured. What went wrong?"

Dex fished around for his tobacco sack and began to make a cigarette. "Too many of you, Barr. Tom in Will's house, some damned fool hunkered out by Will's horseshed — right out where he'd make a target — and all you boys lounging around watching the hitchracks. Too obvious, Barr."

"Yeah?" The sarcasm was cutting. "How come you to leave the grulla horse? He gaunted up?"

"No." Dex lit his cigarette and held out the sack. Barr regarded it dourly, almost sullenly, then begrudgingly took it and started to work on a cigarette of his own. "No, the horse wasn't hurt. Ridden down a little, I reckon the owner'll say, but sound enough. It wasn't that; it was the careless boys with carbines hiding around the grulla. The moonlight shine off their rifle barrels warned me off, there."

Barr didn't speak again until he had his quirley going, then he took a deep inhalation, and let it come out slowly, in a bluish trickle, past his thin lips. He was looking thoughtful. "You were lucky," he said finally.

Dex motioned toward his blankets. "Call it

97

that; it's a good enough name. Personally, I'd say you lawmen got in each other's way. There were too many of you. For some damned reason you're all pretty anxious to get me. Well, be that as it may, there's my sack, Barr; you'd better get some sleep; you look like you need it."

The deputy turned slowly, surveyed the bedroll, strolled over and sat down on it, still smoking and looking at Dex. "You're the first outlaw of any importance we've had in Lovell for a long time, Williams."

Dex squatted. "Nope, not the first. You've got a darn sight bigger one, Barr, only you're too dumb to see it."

"Yeah? Who?"

Dex shrugged. "You'll see in a little while, maybe, if things work out right."

"That's all you'll say?"

"Every darned word; now get some rest. I didn't aim to collect a lawman to ride with me, but I needed you for a shield, back in Lovell; at least I figured I might, so I brought you along. Now I'm glad I did. You'll be back with me when hell breaks loose."

Barr's stare was speculative. "All right; you've got a damned secret. Well, you can keep it. I'll trail along because I got to, but — how about all these hold-ups on the Green Springs stages?"

"I'm guilty," Dex acknowledged, "and I've got the loot to prove it. That satisfy you?"

The deputy stopped his hand in mid-air. He was in the act of dropping the cigarette. "You have what loot?"

"The money I've taken from the Green Springs stages. Got it all cached away."

"The hell you have," Barr said, visibly shaken.

Dex nodded and motioned with one hand. "Go to sleep, will you? We'll be riding pretty soon now, and I don't want to have to tie you on your saddle."

But Barr didn't lie back, not for a long time. He sat there looking at Dexter Williams as though he were some kind of a rare form of life. Never before in his life had the lawman heard of a stage robber who hoarded his loot. What Slim Barr had no idea about, of course, was that Dexter Williams wasn't robbing the Green Springs coaches for wealth, but for revenge against the outfit that had fixed upon him as its personal scapegoat. He finally lay back and stared overhead at the mat of fir boughs. Dex watched him, sitting there relaxed, smoking and thinking back over the night's experiences. And of them all, the one that kept him thoroughly awake in spite of the punishment he'd handed his body over the past twenty-four hours, was Marge Herndon's sudden, forceful kiss in the darkness of the kitchen.

He was still re-living the moment when the sun pushed its way over the grey horizon and worried the chill that was in the air. It burned its way across the breadth of a new day and added warmth to light so that Dex felt himself relaxing over the shoulder where the bunched-up muscles were taut.

"Williams?"

Dex swung his head. "You awake? Good; let's ride."

"Wait a minute. Did Will Herndon know you were coming in to-night?"

"No. Why?"

Barr pushed himself up, spat, cleared his throat and spat again. "Just got to wonderin'. We had a guard watchin' his house."

"I know," Dex said, getting up and dusting needles off his legs. "I was in the house when Tom Bulow came around. Figured from that there was a guard outside. Another tomfool stunt of you lawmen. If you'd come in close and really surrounded the place, you'd of had me."

"I reckon," Barr said, stretching widely, "but old Tom's a funny cuss. He wouldn't let any of us go pokin' around Herndon's place too much."

"Why not? Hell, Herndon's about the only

man in Lovell I know well enough to go see."

"I know that," Barr said wryly, "but Tom said no, so 'no' it was. He's the sheriff — I'm not."

Dex stood in the shade watching the deputy sheriff. He had the definite impression the thin man wasn't nearly as hostile as he was before. "Go get the horses, Barr." He stood watching the deputy comply, trying to gauge the meaning of the man's change; finally he gave it up, and, saddling his animal, swung up and waited. Barr mounted stiffly.

"Damn." He winced from contact with the saddle. "Haven't done much ridin' since I been a town deputy. I'm stiffer'n a ramrod."

Dex jutted his chin. "Head out north-east, Barr. Hold it to a walk unless I tell you otherwise."

"North-east? Where we headin' this time?"

"Don't talk so damned much," Dex shot at him. "Just do like I tell you."

They went along the fringe of trees, never completely leaving their shelter and protection, for a long time. When at last they cut a meadow, Dex lifted the horse into a long lope and nodded at the deputy sheriff. They rode in silence, side by side, until once again the trees closed in around them; then Dex, following the wolf-instincts that had come to be so much a part of him since he'd taken the outlaw trail, cut due east for a craggy over-hang he knew of, where the full panorama of their backtrail would be visible. He let Barr follow, keeping an eye on the lawman but feeling small doubt there was much danger.

When they came out onto the windswept ledge, Dex sucked in his breath with a sharp sound, and Barr looked quickly along the outlaw's line of sight. Far back, coming slowly, undoubtedly having trouble with the tracks through the fir needles that lay like a spongy, fragrant carpet on the forest's floor, was a lone horseman. Oddly, it was Barr who finally spoke.

"Who is he?"

Dex didn't answer; he was too intent in watching the tracker. If the man had been following them all night, and into the new day as well, it would account for the slow progress he was making, for Dex's trail and camp alike were purposefully obscured by the needles. He relaxed a little, thinking.

His hostage made enough inconvenience; if he backtracked, surprised the rider and disarmed him, too, he'd have two prisoners he didn't want, instead of one. If he let the man alone, he'd still have the menace behind him, and that was just as bad. He swore aloud, and let a small look of worry crease his forehead.

"Well?" Barr asked.

"Well, hell. Let him come. I'm not going back after him."

"No? You'll have him behind you then. If he's come this far through those darned trees, it's a good bet he'll find us, eventually."

"Eventually," Dex said savagely, "may make all the difference in the world. Now shut up and let's get going." He reined down off the craggy ledge, rode back into the fringe of trees, and struck out more east than north at a fast walk. Barr followed with a compressed set to his mouth and a mildly-outraged look in his eyes.

The sun marched grandly across the pale sky, adding highlights to the underbellies of the fat little clouds that were up there, visible now and then through the trees. By the time the two riders were riding in a long, gradual decline to the bottomland, where a ribbon of a road lay like a carelessly-cast string, the trees were thinning out and the vast landscape was unrolled endlessly to them from their slight eminence.

Dex studied the road as his horse picked their way downward. There wasn't a sign of vehicular traffic as far as he could see. Far south of them was a lazy, low dust banner that told of riders passing at a slow gait. He kept his attention on this movement until satisfied it held no significance, then ranged his glance over the full extent of the road again.

Slim Barr kneed his horse beside Dex when the trail widened enough to permit it. They were down to the last swell of land by then. "Listen, Williams, I'm not worrying about you, but out here on this prairie we're easy targets for that feller back there in the trees. If you're tired of living, I'm not. Hell, if he lines us up he won't know one from the other."

Dex made a hard smile. "He'll have to have quite a rifle to reach us by the time he comes out of the trees and sees us riding down here."

Barr wasn't convinced, though. "That might not keep him from trying. A man who knows elevations and has a good —"

"Quit worrying, deputy. This is the way we're going, and that feller back there isn't going to change our route. By the time he sees us, we'll be pretty safe, anyway — I hope."

"Well," Barr said sharply, "the least you could do is let me know what's going on."

"You'll see directly."

Dex said no more. His frosty look was sufficient persuasion for the deputy sheriff to subside into inaudible imprecations. He looked back twice as he and Dex rode toward the stage route. The sensation of being the hunted instead of the hunter was a new one

104

to him. He had acute misgivings about the outcome, especially since he no longer had his belt-gun.

But Dex was concentrating on the long stretch of visible roadway. He didn't pay any more attention to the mysterious rider until the lawman swore in a startled, ragged outburst; then he turned and swept their backtrail. Skylined, high on a bony finger of land where the fir trees were a green and brown background, was the horseman. He was silhouetted up there like an Indian. In fact, that's what he reminded Dex of: a buck Indian on the prowl.

"He's seen us, Williams."

Dex nodded. "I reckon he has at that," he said, with deliberate calmness. "Now we'll find out if his gun'll shoot this far."

Barr turned an angry face. "You damned fool —"

"Rope it, lawman." Dex watched the deputy subside into impotent rage, then measured the distance between the unknown pursuer and themselves. The man had evidently made exceptionally good time over the fresh tracks. Dex frowned a little. He had to shake the man, whoever he was. There was a way that occurred to him, but it required a tree. He dropped his glance to the bare plain, sought for and found a scraggly pine that grew alone and lonely, a mile or so south of them. "Come on, Barr. Let's ride over to that pine yonder."

They rode, Barr calming as the gulf between them and the horseman, who was no longer visible on the eminence, widened. When they got to the pine, Dex motioned with his hand.

"Let me have your lariat there."

Wondering, Barr loosened the buckle on the right swell of his saddle and handed the rope over.

Dex nodded. "Now get down."

He tied Slim Barr, with no attention to the blasphemies and worse the lawman heaped upon his head. Finished, he looked at the job, found it satisfactory, took the bridle off Barr's horse, hung it on the saddlehorn, and gave his mount a slap on the rump. The animal turned and struck out for Lovell in a high-headed lope. Dex smiled, and Barr finally ran out of swear words. He was red-faced, and a thick vein stood out at the side of his neck. Dex's smile grew thin.

"You got a choice, deputy. You can stay here and rot, or you can holler out when that feller comes tracking me. It's up to you."

He rode away then, hearing the scorching oaths of the tied lawman and paying them not the slightest heed. He glanced overhead once. The sun was working its way into the position that meant the Green Springs stage wouldn't be far off, if it was on schedule.

The land lay benign and warm. It brought up a drowsiness that Dex had to battle, but in time the warmth became more than pleasant. It turned hot out there in the plain, and he lost his feeling of sleepiness.

The distances were huge and solitary, as the outer banks of heaven must be. Miles of eternity buttoned to the earth and flung back with a grandiose gesture to reveal an endlessness that decades of migration wouldn't dent. He rode over the west side of the road, watching for the telltale dust flags that would presage any travelling vehicle, and saw none. Then he made for a rolling rib of land that had a slight height to it, and reined up on the top of it, waiting.

A lot depended on what came north out of Lovell on the stage road. The future of Dexter Williams, for one thing. A little dream he had been nurturing so carefully, so hopefully against all hope, for the last hurried hours. The dream that had Marge Herndon in it.

He thought of Lovell, and couldn't avoid the hard knot of resentment the town inspired in him now, and yet he still liked the setting. The great range and the slowness of life dependent on the cattle that made up the economy of its environs. He made a cigarette and smoked it stony-faced. There might be a reason for a man to hate and resent the things that had outlawed him, but he couldn't, in any fairness, blame the town for it. He exhaled and looked toward where he knew Lovell was. No; he wouldn't hold it against the town; just the men in it who had made him an outlaw.

Someday, maybe, if things— That was a dust cloud, and a large one. It had to be the first stage. His mouth was dry. The cigarette tasted bitter, like the edge of an alkali sink, where a man might drink because he had to. He cast it away and narrowed his eyes against the glare. The object ahead of the dust was small and indistinct, but it was moving, and fast, too. Travelling north on the way to Mesilla, maybe; at any rate, it wasn't a group of horsemen, he knew that, and no rancher would drive a wagon at that pace. It had to be the stage.

He sat there watching, completely absorbed in the drama of what might lie ahead of him, and didn't hear the faint shout that would be Slim Barr hailing a passing horseman; then he lifted his reins and kneed the horse down off the ledge. It was the morning stage out of Lovell. If things were as he'd tried to make them, there would be a fortune in stolen gold aboard that coach, along with some men whose flinty faces would be watching for a highwayman. And somewhere — God willing — a highwayman would strike.

He was breathing in tight gasps, never letting his glance wander from the careening vehicle, and it was sitting like that, tense all over, that he saw the stage. Made out its outlines easily and recognised it. Saw the glistening span of six horses that drew it like a feather behind them.

He was riding slowly, hunched forward a little, when he swung his head in a slow half-circle, studying the vast expanse of land northward. If the highwayman was going to strike, that single, lonely, drawn-out stretch of road was ideal. Dex could command the full length of it. He let the horse walk aimlessly, paralleling the stage's route, and he didn't glance up once from the fascinating study of the vehicle and the roadway — until the flat, snarling gunshot broke into his thoughts with a venomous whine of lead.

Chapter Four

The bullet came close, but the distance was far too great. Dex swung erect toward the shot. Instinctively he palmed his hand-gun. The effort at delaying the mysterious stranger who had trailed him, by tying Slim Barr to the tree, had failed. The deputy was still tied. The pursuer had ridden callously past him, noting his condition and understanding Dex's purpose. The outlaw was fighting for time now. Was using every ruse he could, to shake the stranger off his trail long enough for him to oversee his trap, laid so carefully with stolen gold.

Dex couldn't make the rider out, beyond seeing that he was tall and gaunt-looking, but he could tell easily enough that the man's horse was just about ridden down. He swore and shot another glance at the stage. It was still approaching them, south-eastward, and evidently the driver hadn't noticed anything unusual in the two small dots that were riders, far ahead and west of the road.

Another carbine shot made Dex turn savagely from his previous preoccupation with the stage, and concentrate on the man who was out to kill him. He knew his most serious disadvantage lay in the fact that he had only a hand-gun to pit against the longer-ranged carbine.

He swung his horse south and lifted him into a slow lope. Twisting in the saddle, he saw the gaunt man kick his own mount into a lope, but the animal handled his legs as though they were leaden. There was nothing handy for cover, either. Dex raged inwardly, watched the carbine come up again, and swerved his horse violently toward the road. The coach was nearly abreast of them. Dex's rage mounted. Caught between two dilemmas, he reined up in a sliding halt, swung back and faced the relentless scarecrow on the dogged horse. His eyes flamed. If the highwayman was in the neighbourhood, he couldn't help but hear the shooting, and only a cursory glance over the naked plain would show him Dex and the gunman, as well as the stage.

He sat there soaked in irrational fury. The highwayman wouldn't strike now. Not with the gunfire and the visible horsemen to scare him off. It was the fault of the man behind him. He swung his horse with a savage tug and lifted his gun, cocked it, then sunk in his spurs. The animal drew on some deep source of reserve energy and leaped out in a wild surge of smooth power. Dex held him straight toward the distant stranger, who was reining up abruptly, apparently in astonishment.

The distance between them closed rapidly. Dex saw the puff of grey smoke before he heard the report. He ignored both, bent lower and squeezed off his first shot. The six-gun made a thunderous bellow that was louder, more deafening, than the flat snarl of the carbine.

Neither shot scored, but Dex saw the lean man swinging down on the off-side of his mount. He pulled back his lips in a cruel smile. The pursuer was on the defensive now. His carbine barrel came twinkling over the seat of the saddle. Dex was within range as he tugged off two fast shots. He had to shoot; the carbine was level and steady.

He had no illusions about the stranger's next shot hitting him or his mount. But before the carbine went off, the horse under it gave a tremendous jump. One of Dex's shots had singed its rump. The rifleman was spun sideways and left fully exposed by his animal's abrupt movement.

He was bringing his gun up again when Dex slid his horse to a halt, flung himself down and fired. The man staggered drunkenly, caught himself, braced his legs wide and shot.

Dex had to roll fast to avoid the plunging,

dying convulsions of his horse. Vaguely he was conscious that the stranger had fired one more shot; then he was limping toward his own mount, which had been shot down and killed.

Dex rolled behind the quivering body of his mount and reloaded the six-gun with oily, shaking fingers. There was a lull, and the silence was oppressive. Somewhere, a man was shouting, but it came from a great distance. He ignored it, assuming the sound came from Slim Barr. Watching, hatless and with his chin against the ground, Dex saw no sign of movement from behind the other dead animal. He was raising his gun to snap off a shot when the carbine roared and the sound of the slug ripping into his flesh bulwark made him wince.

He fired twice, spacing the shots and placing one at each end of the opposite carcass; then he yanked off a third shot, squarely in between the former two, and waited. It was a long, nerve-wracking wait. His hope was beginning to rise when the carbine went off again. Dirt flew knee-high in front of him.

The gunman was holding low. Dex sweated, facing the impasse and crawling with anxiety. The knowledge that his plan was ruined didn't help any. Bitterness flooded him. Bitterness and hatred for the man who was responsible. He had come riding with such high hopes, and now he was pinned down and helpless before a strange gunman, a bounty-hunter more than likely, or some townsman or ranch rider drawn to the chase by the offer of reward money. His scheme was ruined, and so was his little dream. The one that was hope built against hope.

He lay flat, thinking. There was no way out. If he stood up he'd be shot. If he didn't stand out they would have to duel it out, and that could take hours. Anyway, he was afoot now. He thought of Barr's horse and swore again.

Squirming in anguish, he studied the plain on both sides and ahead of him. Behind him lay the stageroad. He didn't look back; there was no reason to. Escape would have to lie over the body of his nemesis, and it would have to be made before riders from some ranch, on their way to Lovell, saw or heard Dex and his enemy.

There was no escape. The land was barren and flat for miles. He looked above, toward the tree-girt uplands, and felt the complete hopelessness of his situation; it brought back the full force of futility and wrath again. He raised up and fired a shot into the dead horse, then dropped flat again. The wait seemed endless, aching for the carbine to answer. It didn't.

Dex squinted around his horse's rump. He

could see nothing. He hefted the six-gun, fired again, and waited. Still no answer. He lay flat and swore, doubting that the gunman was out of the fight and fighting against the inner urge to raise up and take a long look. The minutes went by like oxen; slowly and indifferently and draggingly.

"You over there."

The echo came back, and that was all. Dex ground his teeth. He was in a quandary, and knew it. Was, in fact, more helpless than he'd ever been before, and knew that, too. Then the new sound came into his consciousness, from behind him, and he wrenched himself around and stared. They were coming fanned out, five of them, guns shining in their fists. He stared, recognising Fred Turnbull and both the Bulows, and guessing the other man, the one on the far side of Will Herndon, was the stage driver. He guessed it because the man was carrying a shotgun.

Dex's breath went out like steam under pressure. He could see the deserted coach back a ways, just off the road; then he turned back toward the gunman who was holding him there, and understood. The hidden stranger had an unobstructed view of what was occurring behind Dex. Had no doubt seen the men tumble out of the stage and head for them. Dex smiled bleakly. The stranger's last shot, the one that had thrown dust in front of Dex's dead horse, had been a warning to him to lie low. He was caught between two fires, with the gaunt man holding him there. If he was going to get clear, he'd have to move fast.

He twisted back again. The five stalkers were out of range but moving steadily. He ejected spent casings from his six-gun and reloaded so that the gun was full, then he wiped the sticky sweat off his gun-palm against his shirtfront and got his legs under him. It was all but hopeless. Running, he'd draw fire; staying there, he'd either be killed outright or taken back to Lovell and put in irons and hung, eventually. Even Will Herndon couldn't help him now. The salt-sweat stung his eyes. He swiped at it with a dirty shirtsleeve. If he still had Slim Barr as his hostage . . . but he didn't.

Flexing his legs, Dexter worked them under him, lifted his head a little, and stared over at the other dead horse. There wasn't a sign of movement over there. He sucked in a great, hot breath of air, leaped up and ran. A shout went up far down the land behind him. He kept on running, knowing that his only immediate peril lay in the gunman behind the dead horse; the others were out of gun-range.

The world was a pumping, jumbled kaleidoscope of greys and browns. Dex never took his eyes off the dead horse. Because of that he saw the carbine jerk frantically upwards, slanting towards him. He fired from the hip, saw the slug strike just under the carbine, and frantically fired again.

The two shots were simultaneous, almost. It was as though the carbine blew up in his face. He didn't feel the closeness of the slug because he was running in a stooped, zig-zag pattern; then he saw the tall, gaunt man raise up. The carbine was abandoned, lying barrel down across the dead horse's carcass. There was a six-gun in the man's fist and a twisted, terrible look on his thin face.

Dex recognised him then, just as he fired. It was the red-headed passenger who had survived the highwayman's second attack against the Green Springs company, the man who had stood just outside Will Herndon's saddle-shop and identified Dex Williams as the killer. Then Dex saw the mushrooming explosion like some fantastic, deadly flower blooming, burst from the six-gun's snout. He fired his third shot at the sight, saw the gaunt man stagger once more, take three big steps backwards with a peculiar, off-focus look to his face, then teeter back and forth as though refusing to go down.

Dex stopped wide-legged. It was hard to

breathe. Not hard exactly, but he had to concentrate on doing it or his lungs wouldn't function. There was no sense of pain anywhere; just the strangeness of having to suck air into his lungs through his open mouth.

They faced each other, staring, unblinking and appalled; then the red-headed man coughed. It was a harsh, thick sound. He lowered his head a little and rocked back and forth. Dex came out of his shock like a sleepwalker, raised his gun and felt the dog slipping under his thumb. Something, somewhere inside of him, told him not to shoot again. He let the hammer slide gently until it rested in its niche, then he took his thumb off it. Let the gun sag to his side by its own weight while he watched the man in front of him bend lower, a little lower, head hanging now, scarlet on his chin.

He didn't really fall. It was more like a man kneeling in prayer. Dex was conscious of it that way. The red-head's knees bent slowly, stubbornly fighting to remain stiff. They bent gradually, giving way under relaxing muscles until the man went down, head hanging on his chest, arms at his sides, the six-gun, cocked but unfired, lying in the dust at his side, and his tawny head of hair glinting with dull rust under the pitiless sun.

Then he was down, going forward on his

face, sliding into a shapelessness that had no counterpart in life. Flattened and flat looking, unmoving . . . dead.

Dex's gunhand was moving. He looked away from the drama of death irritably, glanced down at the hand and saw another fist pulling at the pistol in his slack grip. He raised his head and stared into the beautiful, large liquid eyes of Will Herndon. Saw the blank whiteness, the set jaw and churning anguish in his friend's face, and opened his fingers. Will took the gun, held it carelessly and raised his glance to Dex's face. The younger man could see the lips working. It was like hearing the bullet coming before the gun went off. The words came later, indistinctly.

". . . Down, Dex. Sit down."

He saw Tom Bulow staring at him oddly, twisted his head further and watched the sheriff's stocky son coming up close to put a hand out toward him.

"Sit down, Williams, you're hurt."

That was why it was hard to breathe. He was hurt. Dimly he remembered when it had started . . . He blinked at the dead gunman; wanted to swear at him. To curl his lip in scorn because he, Dex Williams, was still standing and the other feller . . .

"Fetch the coach over here, Tim."

He knew that voice, too. It was wheezy,

scratchy, sort of edged with a tinny harshness. Old Frederick Turnbull. He looked at Will Herndon again. "It didn't work, did it, Will?"

" 'Fraid not, son. Here, sit down. Lean back on that horse."

Will's hands forced him down gently. He went without resistance, because defeat came out of nowhere and added its burden to the numbness that was holding back the pain. But when he sat, there was a quick, searing stab of pain somewhere in his body. He gritted his teeth and swore through them.

Faces were in front of him glistening with sweat. Of them all, Tom Bulow's and Will Herndon's alone showed concern. He tried to hold his glance to the wizened old face of Frederick Turnbull, but couldn't.

Hands were plucking at his clothing. It was harder to breathe, he had to unlock his jaws and suck air, then Will Herndon grunted and rocked back on his bootheels. Tom Bulow's face was hidden under his hatbrim. Only Eb Bulow and Frederick Turnbull still stood above him, staring down with absorbed, strained looks, and only Turnbull's showed interest rather than pity.

Dex saw the bloodless lips and the general square look of the old man's jaw. He was able to see the ancient parchment as it had been thirty and more years before. Turnbull senior was a hard, uncompromising, flinty man. Had always been, and would die one. He would value honesty above everything else; above blood, even. It made Dex want to smile.

He saw the coach and six, smelled the odour of the sweaty horses and the scent of the oiled, sun-limp leather, then they were working over him faster, in an aura of strained silence, until finally both Will and the sheriff stood up, ignoring the others and looking at Dex's face intently. The sheriff's mouth was too held-in for him to speak. It was Will who broke the silence.

"Dex? Can you hear me all right boy?"

He nodded. There was a drowsiness coming over him like a fog bank. He felt no desire to answer.

"All right," Will said, "then relax and don't try to help us. We're going to put you into the coach. We won't drop you, son. Just relax and don't strain a muscle. You understand, Dex?"

He heard it and understood, but he didn't want to nod any more. Distantly he heard Tom Bulow speak, but the words faded away.

"Let's wait, Will. He's going out, anyway. Let's wait until he's plumb out; then he won't try to help us lift his weight."

They did. Waited until Dex's head fell forward and his eyes were nearly closed, then they lifted him, the driver, Will and Tom Bulow and Eb, and worked him into the coach while Frederick Turnbull held the door aside. They laid him flat on one seat and hung his legs out the window.

Will crouched low and backed out of the coach. "Mister Turnbull, you mind if we use your coach to haul him back to Lovell?"

The old face pinched up a little. "We could take him on to Mesilla. The stage's on a schedule, Herndon."

"Mesilla's a lot farther, Mister Turnbull." Will's dark eyes were misting over with a sheathed look of violence.

Tom Bulow came up with an apologetic slouch. "Fred, reckon I'll have to commandeer the stage. The law wants him in Lovell."

Turnbull turned his head and regarded Bulow thoughtfully. "Why, Tom? You afraid he'll die? What the hell, man, he's wanted dead or alive. My company'll pay. This is the scheduled Mesilla run, Tom. Won't hurt if he goes there, will it?"

Tom saw the blaze leap up in Will's eyes and moved in quickly, setting his broad bulk between the old man and the saddlemaker. "Sorry, Fred, we're going back to Lovell."

Turnbull didn't argue. He swore and got up into the coach. Will Herndon caught the sheriff's warning glance, ignored it and squeezed past Bulow to take his place beside old Turnbull inside the coach.

Eb Bulow touched his father's arm and jerked his thumb. "How about that dead 'un?"

"Yeah," Tom said indifferently. "You and the driver fetch him over. We'll tie him on top." He stood by the coach door watching the two men struggle under the inert load of the red-headed gunman's body, then helped them boost it onto the top of the coach, where the driver tied it to the luggage rail with a disdainful, displeased look. Tom pushed inside the coach, took a narrow wedge of seat next to Will Herndon. He craned his neck out the window, and when he saw Eb going up over the fore wheel onto the high seat beside the driver, called out for them to drive on.

The drive back to Lovell was made in silence except for a brief conversation between Tom Bulow and Will Herndon when their rag bandage showed warm, fresh blood coming from the ragged flesh beneath it. There was little they could do that they hadn't already done.

Frederick Turnbull sat like a dehydrated old monkey, his leathery hide even darker, more sunburnt and old-looking, inside the coach where there was shade. His small eyes, like chips of faded blue ice, swung irregularly from one to the other of the passengers. He didn't speak until they pulled in by the company office, then he let out a rasping sigh and got down, stamped his feet on the plank walk and waved away a boy who had come up with a wooden paddle and a wooden lard bucket full of black wheel grease.

"No need for that, boy. Fetch Mister Turnbull from inside."

John Turnbull came out with a screwed-up look of bewilderment on his face. Once, his eyes flashed to his father's face then dropped away to watch Sheriff Bulow call to men in the gathering crowd, and motion them to give him a hand in carrying Dex Williams into the sheriff's office, up the road a ways.

The senior Turnbull turned to his son, who was watching the backs of the men carrying Dex. "John, there's that red-headed feller on the top. Fetch him down and have someone pack him over to Newby's shed." The younger man's head jerked around. He stared at his father and didn't move. Annoyed, the old man swore. "Well, move, dammit."

"Is he dead?"

"Yes," the harsh old voice snapped; "he's dead. Deader'n a doggoned skunk. Now get him t'hell off the top o' this coach. There's still a schedule, you know — or do you?"

The news travelled like a grass-fire. Lovell came out of its summer thralldom and hummed with rumours, truths and half-truths. Marge Herndon heard it all, in time, and went breathlessly to the sheriff's office. She was refused admittance, just like the two or three dozen other people who were crowding in close to the solitary window of the office, and around the doors where Eb Bulow stood wide-legged, answering questions automatically, in a strained, dull voice.

Inside, Lovell's sole medical man, Doc Newby, was working over Dex and keeping up a running conversation with the two men who lounged, blank-faced, in chairs. "Looks like the thing went in after it hit his belt buckle. Angled straight up, some darned way — no accounting for a bullet's course, I can tell you that from experience — and stayed just under the hide. Came out near his collarbone, looks like. Funniest thing about wounds like this is that they aren't fatal, not one out of a hundred, unless the man bleeds himself out." Newby straightened up and winced from the bending over. "Who shot him?" He was looking at Tom Bulow when he asked it.

Tom didn't answer. He didn't even look up. Will glanced over at him, read the absorbed look correctly, and spoke. "Red-headed feller. I don't know who he is — was. Maybe Tom does."

"Not many red-heads in Lovell," Newby

said matter-of-factly. "Somebody'll know him."

"John Turnbull might — or Tom, here."

"Huh?" The sheriff's head came up slowly, as though he was pushing his way clear of an unseen obscurity.

"Doc asked what the red-headed feller's name was."

"Oh!" Bulow fished around for his tobacco sack automatically, his eyes still clouded a little with shreds of some deep thought. "Sam Bauman. That's what he told us, anyway. A Texan."

Newby nodded, flexed his arms and bent over the cot again. "Bounty hunter?" he asked.

"Don't know, Doc," Bulow said. "Don't know. That's one of the things that're bothering me."

Will ran a hand along his jaw. "What's bothering you, Tom?"

The sheriff lit up and exhaled a big cloud of smoke, settled deeper in his chair and fixed his glance on the wall over the cot where Dex lay, unconscious.

"Several things. First, what's Bauman doin', trailin' Dex like that?"

"The reward money," Will said dryly. "What else?"

"Naw," Bulow said. "I don't believe that.

126

At least Bauman said he was a cowman when we questioned him after the second robbery. Why'n hell'd a man who was nothing more'n a witness in a killing take it upon himself to ride all over hell's half-acre after a gunman he didn't even know? Reward money? Maybe, Will, but I've been handling men who hunted other men for money for a lifetime, and I've yet to run across a cowman who'd drop his business and take after a man for the bounty."

"Why else, then?"

"Like I just said, I don't know. There's a reason, though, Will. There's a reason, and I've got a hunch if I know what it is I'll have something else interestin' to worry about." Bulow swung his head toward Dex's cot. "Another thing. Why'd this young fool take Slim Barr all over the country with him? Why'd he tell Slim they were going to catch a highwayman?"

Will sighed, looked thoughtfully at Dexter Williams' pallid, still face, and wondered if he dared tell the sheriff of Dex's suspicions. He decided against it, sighed again, and ran a broad finger down the seam of his trousers.

"Will? You know something, don't you?" Tom Bulow's calm, impassive face was a fit background for his blank, unruffled glance.

"Like what, Tom?"

Bulow didn't answer right away. He kept

his emotionless glance on Herndon's face for a few seconds before he spoke. "I don't know, Will. Just something. You think different in this thing than I do. We both know that. Why don't you tell me your side of it?"

"Can't, that's why." Will jutted his chin toward the cot. "It's up to Dex. If he wants to tell you anything, that's his business. I won't say a thing."

"Not even to save his bacon, Will?"

The saddlemaker swung his head. The old danger signals were flying like battleflags in his dark, handsome eyes. "I'll do anything I can to save his hide, Tom, anything. But *he'll* have to tell you what we think — not me."

"Ummm," the sheriff said drawlingly, looking back at the cot just as Newby straightened up for the second time, and arched his back a little and made a face. "Suppose he doesn't pull out of it, Will. What then?"

Newby went to a little basin on the cold woodstove and began to wash his hands. He spoke without looking around. "Oh, he'll pull out of it all right, Tom. It'll take time, but he'll make it all right. You got no worry there."

"How long'll it take?" Will asked.

Newby shrugged. "Depends, Will. He's built like a stud-horse. If he's got the stamina to go with the build, I'd say maybe a month;

128

maybe even less. You can't tell. Too many things to be considered, like strength, healing power, guts, will, and the like. But I'll give you odds he'll make it all right. The main thing to watch for now is infection. Keep the thing clean and freshly bandaged, and a nickel's worth of luck'll do the rest."

The doctor turned and eyed them both, drying his hands. "Who do I bill for this job?"

Will's anger came up again. He controlled it, but just barely. "Bill me — Shylock," he said acidly.

Newby shook his head back and forth disapprovingly. "Will, I'm surprised at you. You make saddles for nothing?"

"Cut it out," Tom Bulow said, arising from his chair with an annoyed look. "Thanks a lot, Doc. Will's a mite upset is all; he didn't mean that." Bulow crossed the room and stood over the cot looking down. An uneasiness gripped him. "Doc? You sure about this? He looks more'n half-dead to me right now."

Newby was shrugging into his coat. He walked over and looked at Dex with a professional coolness, then smiled. "Sure, Tom. He'll be all right. They all look like that when they've bled a lot and are unconscious." Newby's brows drew in a little. "But I'd like to make a suggestion. When he's able, feed the hell out of him. Being on the dodge has just about fleshed him out."

"Yeah," the sheriff said absently, then turned to face the medical man. "Doc, there's that red-head atop the stage —"

"I reckon they've taken him to my shack by now, Tom. I'll give him a good going over before I plant him. You want the stuff, as usual?"

"Yeah. Clothes and all, Doc. There's something funny about that feller."

Newby nodded and turned toward the door. He shot Will Herndon a fast, tentative glance, got a wooden stare and a slow nod, repaid it in kind, then went out. Eb Bulow took the door and pulled it firmly closed behind him.

Bulow turned away from the cot and regarded Will in silence; then he slumped, throwing all his weight on one foot. "Will, when you asked me to ride that stage and guard your money, I did it." Herndon didn't move his glance from the floor. "Sure," the sheriff went on in his quiet tone, "that's my job. But you know I didn't have to do it myself. I could've sent Eb. That was a favour. Now you do me one. Give me the stuff you've got kegged up inside o' you."

Will arose. "Sorry, Tom. Can't do it." He nodded toward Dex. "It's his secret, not mine. Maybe he'll tell you."

Tom Bulow came close to a frown. "Well, tell me the truth now. Was Williams in your place last night?"

"Yeah."

"And he was in the root cellar, wasn't he?"

"Yes. You didn't say it, but I knew what you were thinking when you looked out the transom window down there, Tom."

Bulow dropped and stomped out his cigarette. "Will, you were obstructin' justice."

"The hell I was," Will flared at him. "Not justice, Tom. The law maybe, but not justice."

"You're pretty sure Williams isn't an outlaw, aren't you?"

Will shrugged. "Like you said one time, Tom. Men get to know one another pretty well, after a while."

"What's that mean?"

"I know what you're thinking. You think, because Dex robbed the Green Springs stages he was an outlaw."

"Well," Bulow snorted, "wasn't he?"

"Sure he was. He'll tell you that himself. But he didn't have a hand in the office robbery or the first stage holdup, either. And he told me that every dime he's taken from the Turnbull stages he's got cached away."

"Yeah," the sheriff said, "he told Slim Barr that, too. That's another funny thing, isn't it?"

"Very funny," Will said, crossing to the

door, putting his hand on the lift and turning back to face the sheriff again. "Funny as a gut-shot, Tom. He wants to give that money back. I tried to talk him into it. So'd Marge. You know why he wouldn't? Because he said neither you nor Turnbull'd let him off if he did."

Tom Bulow's steady glance held to the door, where it had closed behind the saddlemaker. His mouth was open to say something, but he closed it when Will stormed out of the little office. Slowly, he turned and looked down at the unconscious outlaw. "Funniest damned renegade I ever run across, Williams. You sure as hell are."

Tom Bulow went to the door, opened it, saw the lingering loafers, and crooked a beckoning finger at Slim Barr, who was trying to ward off more questions. "Come in here, Slim."

The deputy entered the office, shot a startled glance at Dex, and swallowed hard. "Is he dead, Tom?"

"No, not yet. Doc says he won't die, but he sure looks dead to me."

"Yeah," the deputy said, staring.

"Sit down, Slim. Now tell me what happened."

The deputy began at the beginning and told his story. Even recounted the conversations as best he could, word for word, and drained himself of all he knew. Tom Bulow listened without showing anything in his face. When Barr was finished, the silence between them grew and grew and grew. Barr squirmed uncomfortably, waiting. Finally, the sheriff shot a question.

"He give you a hint who this highwayman was?"

"No; he always dropped the subject or told me to shut up when I got close to asking."

More silence. Bulow was stumped. He looked at the unconscious man and wished with all his might he could penetrate Dex's secret. "You talked with Bauman, Slim. What do you think of him showin' up, trackin' you and Williams?"

Barr was touched in the quick that time. He looked puzzled and uncertain. "I can't make head or tails out o' that, Tom. Damned if I can. No one was more surprised than I was when I saw who that was, trailin' us. What's stumped me ever since was the way he looked over at me as he rode by — like he'd never seen me before — then kept right on riding after Williams. Can't figure that out."

"I can," Sheriff Bulow said. "I can figure that much out all right, Slim. Bauman may have been a cowman like he told us he was

— and maybe he was a doggoned liar, too. But when he bypassed you, that was the same as sayin' he was after just one thing: Dexter Williams. Why would he be after Dex? Well, for the reward money; what the hell else? He didn't know Dex personally. He didn't know the man Dex is supposed to have killed on the stage with him. He couldn't have had but one purpose, Slim. Bounty money."

Slim Barr nodded his head slowly. "I believe that, Tom. I believe it for a different reason, though. I was close enough to see them fight. Bauman was a gunman. Maybe he was a cowman, too; I don't know. But I *do* know that he was a gunman. I've seen enough of 'em — watched 'em handle their guns — to know one when I see him."

"Uh-huh," Tom Bulow said. "We've got this much of it figured, then. Bauman was a gunman and a bounty hunter. That means he probably wasn't any cowman. It also means he lied to us to hide his real occupation and — talent." Bulow's eyes were drawing into a slight pucker. "You know what else that means, Slim? It means he was hired to get Dexter Williams."

The deputy was looking at his employer with an intent regard. The sheriff went on speaking, but softly, though he was thinking aloud, not addressing anyone in particular.

"So he was a gunman. A hired gunman. Who hired him, and why? I don't know, but I'm beginning to think maybe Dexter Williams isn't alone in this mess. Beginning to look to me like maybe he isn't more'n just one of the men we want, and not a very important renegade at that." The sheriff slapped his chair arm and stood up. "Slim, go get Marge Herndon. She can take over the nursing of Dex. Unless I'm blind as well as dumb, she won't object. Go on."

Barr left the office with something like excitement coursing through him. He, too, had come to the reluctant conclusion that Dexter Williams didn't strike him as the dangerous renegade he was supposed to be; not after they had ridden together, talked together on that long ride before the final disaster.

But Marge wasn't home, and Slim puzzled over that. He continued to be puzzled until he went back toward the sheriff's office and saw her coming toward him from the direction of Doc Newby's house; then he understood with a rare flash of intuition, which was something that happened only a couple of times in his life.

"Miss Herndon, the sheriff wants you to sort of look after Williams, ma'm, if you will."

Marge's liquid glance made Barr's heart skip a beat. "That's where I was going. Taking this — these things to Tom's office. They belong to that man who was killed."

Eb admitted them with a bored glance that lit up briefly when he met Marge's glance; then he closed the door behind them to continue his guard duty against the thinning ranks of the curious who still hung around. They were hoping for a glimpse or a word that would be official; a wonderful basis for fabrications of gossip built on half-truths.

Sheriff Bulow took the bundle from Marge and thanked her, then rolled his head sideways on his shoulders toward Dex's cot. "Marge, would you mind looking after him? He looks worse'n he is, the Doc says, an' I thought you —"

"Dex!" She crossed the room and knelt beside the cot. Slim Barr and the sheriff exchanged startled glances, writhed in embarrassment and turned their attention to the bundle Newby had sent up from the dead man. They tried ignoring Marge completely, even to the extent of attempting to close out the little animal sobs she couldn't quite stifle.

"Here's his purse, Tom."

Bulow spoke without looking up. He was studying Bauman's clothing intently. "Anything in it, Slim?"

"No money; Just some papers."

"Wouldn't be any money," the sheriff said

caustically, looking up. "Wish I was a doctor with an undertaker's job on the side. Pickings must be pretty good. What's that?"

Barr passed over the crumpled paper. Tom laid it out flat on the tabletop and smoothed it out. Pencilled words in a cramped scrawl looked up at him. "Looks like directions of some kind, Slim. You're younger — got better eyes. See what you make of it."

Barr bent over the paper. His mouth formed words with painstaking effort, then he straightened up with a shrug. "Don't make sense to me. Says 'Hannibal and Carthage' something or other."

The sheriff was finished with the clothing. He didn't comment as he looked through the purse, found nothing but some small change, and looked disinterestedly at the pocket-knife and stub of a pencil that were all Bauman had had in his pockets. "Hannibal and Carthage. Beats me. Never heard of either of 'em, did you?"

"No," the deputy said, thoroughly mystified. "I don't know whether they're men or towns."

Marge Herndon turned her head a little. "They're towns in Missouri."

Tom looked over at her, studied the length of her back unseeingly, then nodded. "That's it, Slim. Bauman's from Missouri. At least he was there. I'll send off a letter to the sheriff of these towns."

"It's better'n nothing," Barr said, without much hope. "I'm about done in, Tom. If you don't need me any more, I'd like to get some sleep."

"Go ahead. See you in the morning."

Marge arose from beside Dex's bed, pulled over a chair and sat in it. Her eyes were ringed with a blue, worried look. "Tom? Who was that red-headed man?"

"Danged if I know, Marge. Sure like to know, though." Bulow glanced at Dex's profile. "How's the patient?"

Marge's hands were like dying birds in her lap. She glanced back down at the outlaw's face, and Tom Bulow, seeing her profile, felt a lump in his throat he hadn't experienced in twenty-five years. "I wish I knew, Tom. I wish I knew."

She didn't know until several hours later, when Dex came out of his somnolence; and ever after that, for two days, Marge worried; but Dex himself allayed her fears by having a ravenous appetite, and on the third day he kissed her. She turned scarlet because both of the Bulows were in the office. Her back was to them, but she knew they had seen and were nonplussed. They had been talking; then the room filled up with a shocked silence.

After a while Tom muttered gruffly; then he and his son left the office and they were alone.

"Honey," Marge said, half-jokingly, half-sincerely, "you're making an old woman out of me."

Dex smiled. "If you'd shave me, Marge, you could see how I've aged, too. I must look a hundred years old underneath this mesquite shrubbery."

She looked at him owlishly. "But I've never handled a razor before, Dex."

He smiled up at her. "If I'm to get my throat worked over anyway, I'd sooner have you do it with a razor than Bulow with a rope."

"Don't talk like that!"

"Will you do it?"

She nodded with a dubiousness that made him chuckle. "I'll try, Dex."

She shaved him. It took a full hour and a minimum of bloodshed, but she did it. Dex ran a hand over his cheek. It felt feverish, but smooth. "Thanks, Marge. Don't throw that razor away. You may have to do it again, sometime."

"I won't; it's dad's razor."

Dex looked up at her. "Where is Will? I'd like to see him."

"He said he'd be over in the morning."

And he was, but not as Dex expected him to be. He burst into the sheriff's office like a tornado. Dex and Tom Bulow both swung to face him.

"Tom, the stage safe was looted again!"

Bulow blinked once, his sole concession to astonishment. "The hell you say."

"Yeah; John just told me."

Tom got up with an oath. "Why didn't he tell me? I'll go see him." At the door he turned back and fixed Will with a hard stare. "I suppose your money's in Mesilla all right, isn't it?"

"I reckon. I'll go up and pick it up in the next few days."

"Yeah," the sheriff said, flicking a glance at Dex and Marge before he went out, and slammed the door irritably behind himself.

Dex was watching Will Herndon. The saddlemaker's face had a worried look to it. "Will? What'd John say?"

"Something about the safe being rifled. T'tell you the truth, I didn't listen too closely. It just startled me too much."

"Why?" Marge asked.

Will shrugged, frowned and pulled up a chair. "Well, for one thing, there couldn't have been as much in it as six thousand dollars; so why'd he rob it again when more money was at hand over in Mesilla?"

Dex stared at the ceiling. "Maybe it was too long a ride."

"Maybe," Will said, then changed the subject. "How d'you feel, son?"

"Good enough," Dex answered. "Maybe I'll get up in a few more days." He was watching Marge's face when he said it. She straightened in her chair.

"You will not. Doctor Newby said —"

"That old fraud," Will growled.

Marge turned on him with a savage look that surprised both Dex and her father, but she didn't speak because Sheriff Bulow came back into the office with a strange look on his face. He crossed the room slowly, sluggishly, and stood over them, looking straight at Will Herndon. The saddlemaker's brow wrinkled.

"What's the matter, Tom?"

"Nothing much, Will. Nothing much. Only you misunderstood John. He didn't say the Lovell office's safe was rifled. He said the Mesilla office's safe was robbed. That means your six thousand dollars more'n likely is gone."

Dex was the first to break the thick silence. He was looking up at the sheriff with a sardonic smile. "Couldn't have been me that time, could it, sheriff?"

Bulow didn't answer. He just stood there with that carefully-maintained blankness of his, made a cigarette, lit it and puffed twice on it before he spoke. "Dex, you and Will know something. You two've got something up your sleeve. Well, now, listen to me. You're in a bad spot. Even if you make full restitution to Turnbull's company, you're still a renegade in the eyes of the law. I'm paid and sworn to prosecute outlaws, no matter what they do — legal or illegal — but I'm going to make you a proposition. You tell me all you know or suspect about this damned business, and I'll promise you, if it helps me catch a highwayman and a safe robber, I'll do everything I can under the sun to get the charges against you dropped. A clean pardon for you, Dex, in exchange for some information."

Dex listened without appearing to. His glance was on the ceiling again. It didn't move when he spoke, either. "Let me think it over, sheriff. It's not as simple as that."

"Why isn't it?"

Because the news gets around. As soon as you'd move, the hombre I've got it in for would run out like a cut calf."

"Oh, no he won't," the sheriff said grimly. "I'll have him locked up so fast he'll never have time to figure out what's happened."

Dex's glance went to the impassive face. "That's just what I don't want to happen. You lock him up and he'll be out the same hour. I want him tripped up legally, with his hands full of stolen money."

"All right," Bulow said, chopping the air with a brusque nod. "I'll ride the river with you on that."

"Thanks," Dex said dryly, "but I want to think it over. I'll let you know."

Sheriff Bulow turned his attention to Will Herndon. "You'd better talk some sense into him, Will. That was your six thousand, you know."

Will didn't speak. None of them did until long after Tom Bulow left the office again and they were alone. Then it was Marge, not her father, who spoke first.

"Dex, let him help you."

"I will, honey, but not until I've got it all figured out. Right now, all we have to do is get him suspicious of John Turnbull, and he'd lock him up. Know what'd happen next? Old Fred Turnbull'd have a lawyer get John out within an hour. That'd warn John off, get the old man sore as a boil, and defeat exactly what we don't want defeated."

Will stared gloomily at the wall. "Yeah," he said absently, with no spirit in his voice. "And if we're wrong in our suspicions — or if some other renegade robbed that safe, Dex — you won't be able to pay back what you've taken from the Green Springs company, either."

Dex hadn't thought of it that way. It made small beads of perspiration come out on his upper lip. Marge was watching him like a hawk. She leaned forward and brushed her father's arm lightly. "Dad, go lock up the shop. I'll be along in a little while."

Will glanced over at her, read the plea in her face, and got up heavily; touched Dex's shoulder awkwardly, self-consciously, with his fingers, and went out. When they were alone, Marge dropped to her knees beside the cot and kissed Dex on the mouth. She used a ridiculous little handkerchief to wipe away the perspiration on his face, and smiled at him.

"Don't you trust Tom, honey?"

He smiled at her. "Well, in a way, yes. But Marge, I'm still an outlaw, remember. Tom Bulow would listen to what I told him, then do exactly what he wanted to do. That would spoil the show for all of us. He needs a prisoner badly. No one knows that worse than he does. He wouldn't be content to sit back and wait, I don't think."

She was watching his face as he spoke. It wasn't that she wanted him to give in to the demands of the sheriff so much as a very natural desire she had to see him out of his trouble. In the final analysis, however, she would

144

concede to him. Her primary concern had been over his health. Now that he was well on the road to recovery, she was more than glad of her role as hospitaler, and in that role, he admitted privately, she had no peer.

He lay there thoughtful and aware of her presence; then eventually he turned and looked up at her. "Marge — would you marry me? That wasn't what I was going to say, but — would you?"

"I not only would, Dex; I will."

He smiled. It was a gentle, almost sad smile. "Not yet, Marge, but one day. One day, darling, and soon, I hope."

"You don't hope it any more than I do," she said fervently.

"Then do me a favour. Ask Will to ride up to Mesilla and act as though he was mad about the loss of his six thousand dollars, will you? Ask him to inquire around; see if he can discover whether John Turnbull was in Mesilla the day or night of the robbery."

"All right, dear, but what about Lovell? Wouldn't it be wise to ask around here, too?"

Dex shook his head. "I don't think so. The less we say around Lovell the better. So far I'm the outlaw — the renegade — as far as folks know. Let's let 'em go on thinking that. If Turnbull gets an idea that I'm not his scapegoat, he'll get suspicious, and that's what we don't want. Understand, Marge?"

"Yes, dear, but what can my father find out up at Mesilla? It isn't likely that they'll know much about John there, is it?"

"Maybe not, but we've got to try it, anyway."

"And if nothing comes of that — what then?"

Dex felt slightly aggravated, but he kept it from his face. She was anxious and worried. Both the men she loved were involved in something that might burst out into gunfire at any moment. He reached up and touched her face. She was lovely. It made a thick knot under his heart, just looking at her; seeing the fear that shone with a steady, undiminishing light, out of her eyes.

"Let's not worry about that yet, Marge."

She nodded without speaking, leaned over and kissed him. A long, soft kiss. The kind that meant more than words could say. He understood it that way, and so did she, but when she straightened up and spoke, it was to say something that astonished him, then made him want to laugh out loud. It showed that she wasn't all softness. There was a shrewdness behind those gorgeous dark eyes, too.

"Dex, there's only one door to the sheriff's office. The front one. And Dex, Tom has a guard out there day and night."

He nodded up at her very solemnly. "He told me that, Marge. I reckon he thinks a little like you do. That maybe now that I'm getting strong again, I might decide to ride out of here."

She coloured. "I just thought I'd tell you. Good night, Dex."

He watched her cross the room and close the door; then he raised up and grinned. Was still grinning when Tom Bulow came in and slammed his hat on the table, swore with more feeling than Dex had ever seen the sheriff display before, and turn a baleful glance toward the cot.

"Damn it all, Dexter, you're balkin' the law."

Dex nodded at the angry flush in the lawman's face. "Sure am, sheriff. You can't hang me any higher for killing ten men than you can for killing one, can you?"

"What're you talking about?"

"I won't get into any more trouble for withholding information from you now than I'm already in as a stage robber."

Bulow sat down heavily in his chair and worked at controlling the exasperation that showed in his normally impassive, calm, unruffled face. "But why? Don't you want to get out of this mess?"

"Do you think there's a chance?"

"Damned if I know. All I know for sure is that Fred Turnbull's after me to try you right away. To fetch a judge in here from the capitol and have you tried."

"For robbery?"

"No; for murder."

Dex tensed. "He's out for blood, that old devil."

"What'd you expect? He had a witness that you killed that doggoned passenger, and you killed his witness. He wants you tried before folks forget what the witness said. He's gone and rounded up ten or twelve men who heard Bauman say you were the killer."

"He isn't going to press the robbery charges, is that it?"

Bulow swore again, in disgust that time. "Why should he? If you're hung for murder he'll have more satisfaction than he'll get out of seeing you sent back to prison for five years or so. He's out for your hide, boy, so if you know anything that'll keep it from being nailed to the barn door, you'd better let me have it. Maybe I can help you."

"Thanks," Dex said dryly, and lay back again, his head cradled in his arms. "I don't suppose you'd take my parole, would you?"

Bulow's blank face swung to bear on Dex's profile. "Not on your life. You'd ride out of here and I'd never see you again."

"My word's better'n that, sheriff."

"Maybe so, but maybe old Fred wouldn't think so. He used to be a one-man posse with a hangrope on his saddle. I wouldn't trust him as far as I could throw him, even yet. He'd get you sure as shootin'."

Eb Bulow came in, flashed a glance at his father, then looked speculatively at Dex. "I'll spell you now, dad." Tom Bulow got up with a grunt, nodded to his son, and left the room. Dex turned his head and saw the level, distrustful glance Eb had him pinioned with. It made him smile. He remembered the first time they'd met in Will's saddle shop.

"Fetch some cards, Bulow. We can have a hand."

Eb wagged his head firmly. "No thanks. I'll just sit over here and you stay in your bed. We'll get along fine that way."

Dex laughed softly. The younger Bulow made a slightly amused, wry grin back at him. "Can't afford to make the same mistake twice, Dex. Feller could get hurt doin' that too often."

Dex lay back again. "All right," he said. "I don't blame you, but I don't think I'm going to have to do that again."

Bulow didn't answer. He pulled a chair over against the front wall, laid his six-gun in his lap, tilted his hat back and shoved the bolt to the front door. He was set for the night. Dex turned on his side and tried to sleep. It came, but not for a long, torturous hour, and in the meantime the legion of doubts assailed him. Especially the glum idea that Will had about someone beside John Turnbull robbing the Mesilla office and making off with that six thousand dollars.

If that were true, Dex was in a fix. He didn't think it possible, yet John Turnbull wasn't the only highwayman around either, and the possibility of a leak through Green Springs company employees was quite possible.

When Dex slept, it was fitfully, uneasily, and with the coming of dawn he was wide awake and grunting at the drowsy deputy who was still tilted back against the front wall of the office, his eyes red-rimmed and blood-shot-looking.

"Say, Bulow; have you heard of any more highwaymen around the country lately?"

"Besides you? No, and if you want the rest of it I'll give you that, too. I hope to hell no more show up until I get caught up on my meals and my sleep."

"How about that Mesilla robbery? Up there at the stage office."

"Yeah, dad told me about that. We'll have to make the ride, I reckon. There's got to be an investigation." The lawman cleared his throat. "I wish to hell you renegades'd go to bigger towns for your plunder. Lovell's too quiet. There isn't enough money around here to keep you happy, long."

"No? Well, I've done all right around here."

"And what'd it get you?"

"Shot a couple of times, and in jail, but you said it didn't pay in these sleepy little towns. I say it does. But what bothers me is this Mesilla robbery."

"Why? You mad 'cause some other owl-hoot's breakin' into your territory?"

Dex rolled his head and squinted a long look at the bleary-eyed deputy. "You're like a bull with buckshot in his rear this morning. Why don't you go get some shut-eye?"

"Will, as soon as Slim or Tom show up."

Dex fell into a prolonged silence. He considered the Mesilla robbery again. Examined it from all angles and came up with the same conclusion he'd had before. John Turnbull knew about the money. For some reason he hadn't dared fake another safe robbery at the Lovell office, and beyond a doubt, if he'd figured on robbing the stage en route, Dex's gunfight with Bauman had scared him off. That, or Turnbull junior was wily enough to make his robbery against the Mesilla office this time, thus striking where he'd never robbed before and avoiding a lot of risk that way.

Dex squinted at the ceiling. John Turnbull, wooden-expressioned, taciturn and a lone wolf, made a mighty slippery enemy and a mighty clever one. He thought back to how deftly he, Dex, had been manœuvred into jeopardy the first time. It was handled with finesse all right. He'd hand Turnbull that much credit. And now, even though the law knew he hadn't committed the Mesilla theft, he was still up to his neck in trouble, and wounded to boot, all because of the elusive John Turnbull.

He recalled the determination he'd had the night he stole the horse and took Slim Barr with him. He was going to force John Turnbull out into the open. Make him fight as Dex was fighting, with his guns as well as his wits. But how?

" 'Morning, Eb. 'Morning, Williams."

Dex looked over at the lean, gaunt height of deputy-sheriff Slim Barr. He didn't answer. Didn't have to, nor get the chance, either, for Eb Bulow was grumbling in a steady monotone. Barr nodded sympathetically and took over the chair, made a cigarette, and held up the sack as the sheriff's son went out and slammed the door.

Dex shook his head. "No, thanks. Later, maybe."

Barr lit up and smoked with a slight grin. "Looks like you'n me'll have the place to ourselves to-day."

"Yeah? How's that?"

Barr tested the slant of the chair, then leaned back in it and exhaled. "Tom got routed out of bed before dawn this mornin'. Some darned fool went and shot a dance-hall girl over on the Flats."

"The Flats?" Dex asked vaguely. "Where's that?"

"Messican town about ten, twelve miles west o' us. Used to be a great rustler hangout in the early days. Now it's just a gamblin' town with a few tumble-down adobes and a flock of border riff-raff."

Dex saw the persisting little half-smile around Barr's mouth. It made him curious. He knew the deputy was keeping the best until the last. "All right; what's the rest of it?"

"Witnesses say John Turnbull did the killing."

Dex froze where he lay, staring at the lawman's widening grin.

Chapter Five

If John Turnbull had indeed shot some dance-hall girl, he'd had a good reason. Dex tried to fit it into Turnbull's outlaw activities, and it wasn't hard to do. Turnbull wasn't the first, by a long shot, nor would he be the last, who had robbed and killed and betrayed over a woman.

He made an ugly grimace. Was that why he needed that money? Some little tramp was taking him down the line. Bleeding him of every dime he could beg, borrow and steal. It was an old story. So old Dex marvelled at a man like Turnbull falling for it. And yet, when he recalled the smooth, soft face of old Fred's son, with its cold, introverted look, its secretive eyes and unfriendly expression, he could see where John Turnbull would be the kind of a man who might become involved, just as he could be the type who'd kill indiscriminately.

Dex remembered what Will had said of young John. He would kill if he had to; and Will should know. If his surmise was correct, then he had the answer to Will's question of why Turnbull junior had robbed his father's company to the point of ruin. Over a dance-hall girl! Dex shook his head in scorn.

"Slim? What else do you know about the killing?"

"That's all. Just that the Mex constable from over at the Flats rode in here before dawn and routed old Tom out. Tom come by my place and told me he was sendin' Eb to Mesilla to investigate this other business — the stage robbery — and he was ridin' for the Flats an' for me to stay here and watch you."

"The constable didn't give him anything more'n that?"

"He didn't say, Dex. He was madder'n a boiled owl, and I don't blame him. He hasn't had much sleep lately."

"Yeah."

They were both drenched in silence, each busy with their own thoughts, when Marge came in with Dex's breakfast. Dex told her of the killing while he ate. She asked questions of deputy Barr with a round-eyed look, then sat staring at the floor until Dex finished and, pushing the tray aside, looked up at her.

"Honey? Has Will gone already?"

"Yes. He left about sunup."

Dex felt like swearing. He wanted Will to do something else for him. He had another plan. Now he'd have to use Marge, and he didn't like having to do it. He didn't want to get her involved any more than she was. A glance at Barr showed him watching them both with considerable interest. Dex wanted to talk to Marge. He didn't dare with the deputy listening in. His wandering glance fell on an old pen on the sheriff's table. He brightened.

"Honey, will you hand me that pen?"

She reached over and got the thing, handed it to Dex and watched him begin to write on a scrap of paper he took from the wallet in his trousers. He wrote fast, finished with a flourish, and turned the paper so Marge could read it. She ran several quick glances over the lines, shot him a wondering look, then re-read it. Slim Barr's chair came off the wall with a screeching sound. Dex looked up. The lawman was standing, scowling down at him.

"What you doin', Dex?"

"Writin' things for Marge to read that I dassen't say in front of you. Things that are better said between a man and the woman he's in love with. You mind?"

Barr lost a little of his suspicious look, but not too much of it. "Well," he said, doubtfully, "don't make any faults. I'm watchin' you like a hawk, remember that."

Marge reached for the little paper, took it in her fist and put it down the front of her

156

dress. Dex smiled at her. She was looking a mute question, but she said nothing.

"Thanks, honey. Let me know, will you?"

She got up, took the wooden tray and nodded. "In a little while."

Both men watched her walk out; then Barr made a cigarette and smoked it. The suspicion was almost gone, but not quite. "You're pretty slippery, Dex. You've made a monkey out of Eb and me both. I don't aim for it to happen again, so watch yourself."

"Don't worry, Slim. I'm sorry about you and Eb. In Eb's case I thought I'd better do that — get clear of the law before I got high-graded back to prison. In your case, I wanted a witness to something that should've cleared me of a lot of the trouble I'm in. It didn't work out, is all."

"Well," Barr said dourly, "no more notes and stuff like that from now on. You got something to say — come out and say it — even to Marge."

"Sure. How about some tobacco?"

Barr tossed the sack over and watched Dex roll a cigarette. They were both smoking an hour or so later when Marge returned. Her face was pale but her eyes sparkled. Dex looked at her inquiringly, and she nodded.

"Worked out, did it?"

"Dex —" She glanced at the lawman,

frowned at his suspicious stare, then nodded vigorously. "Yes; oh yes!"

Dex glanced sardonically at Barr. The deputy was definitely aroused. He glared accusingly at the renegade. "Dex, I don't believe what you told me."

"You don't have to; not now. Forget it."

Barr's scowl got blacker, but he held his silence. Marge reached down quickly and held Dex's hand in a tight, excited grip. Her face was eloquent with meaning. He understood. What she had done for him had worked out better than Marge had expected. He winked very solemnly and jerked his head toward the door.

"See you later, honey. If Will gets back before dark, ask him to come over, will you?"

She nodded, and gave his hand a hard squeeze. She stood up and smiled down at him, then turned and left the sheriff's office. Dex threw back his covers and swung around facing Barr. The deputy's glance was more surprise than anything else. Dex grinned, reached for his clothing and laboriously clothed himself, used the wall as a prop, and stood up. The effort made pinwheels of dizziness race around inside his head. He had to lean against the wall with a fixed, foolish smile, and blink at the diminishing gyrations of the room. Barr was sitting motionless, one hand held out in front of him, unconsciously.

"Take it easy. You'll fall. Better sit down, dammit. I don't want anything to happen to you while I'm on duty."

Dex kept his fixed smile. There was perspiration on his face. "I'm weak — like a cat. Be all right directly."

But it took almost an hour of steady trying before he could stand up without the aid of the wall, and even then he couldn't take more than a few steps at a time before the dizziness returned in a rush. Barr, meanwhile, was offering a little encouragement and advice. It was as though he sympathised with Dex's shakiness and wanted him to overcome it. A natural reaction for a well man toward one who wasn't well.

"Move toward the table. Don't get out in the middle of the room. Keep the cot or the table close to hand, Dex. That's it. You'll make it. Set for a spell, now. Get a little rest before you try it again."

Dex sat, and the weakness went down into his legs until they felt like they were made of soft cotton. He rubbed them a little, bending over to do it. "Hell of a note. Strange what lyin' in bed'll do to a man, isn't it?"

"Yeah," Barr said, "but it takes time to come back, too. You want to remember that. Take it slow for a few days, then you'll be as good as ever."

Dex shot him a saturnine look. "If I get too good, Slim, the law'll lock me in one of those cells over there. Better just to be sick."

Barr blinked at him. Some of the enthusiasm slid off his face and a slow thoughtfulness replaced it. "That's right, too. Tom'll lock you in as soon's you're able. Come to think of it, Dex, maybe I hadn't ought to let you wander around."

"No law against me getting my strength back, is there?"

Barr shrugged. "No, but you'd better just walk around that half of the room."

Dex laughed at him. "Slim, I couldn't beat my way out of a paper sack right now, let alone risk jumping you. Forget it."

Barr was reassured. There was no doubt about Dexter's weakness. He settled back and watched Dex exercise, offering occasional advice, until Marge came with the noon meal. While he ate, she looked at the deputy with a wondering glance.

"Why didn't the sheriff lock John Turnbull up, Slim?"

"Darned if I know, unless it's because he wants to check the Mex constable's story first. After all, Mexes lie pretty easy, Marge, and the Turnbulls aren't men a body wants to mess around with unless he's got 'em dead to rights.

160

Why? D'you see John around town?"

Marge nodded. "Talked to him a little while ago, down by the stage office."

"He act nervous?"

"I suppose you could say so, but John's always been a difficult person to understand."

"Yeah," the deputy said dryly, "like a stone." He shrugged. "Tom'll be back before long, I'd figure. It isn't far over to the Flats."

But Barr was wrong. Tom didn't come back until the late shadows were falling, and by that time John Turnbull had come to the sheriff's office first. Slim Barr let him in past the bolted door with a frank look of surprise on his face.

"What you want, John?"

The stage company manager's face was as emotionless-looking as his words were lifeless. "Want to talk to Williams for a minute, Slim."

He was admitted, but Barr's wariness was back, compounded as he stood with his back against the re-locked door, staring at the two of them. Dex showed no surprise at the visit. In fact, he showed nothing at all in his glance or expression.

Turnbull was big and fleshy and stolid-looking. It was a natural deception. He wasn't stolid; just wasn't talkative or expansive. He stood by the sheriff's table and stared down at Dex.

"Williams; they tell me you got all that money you stole from us."

"Who told you?"

The grey eyes flickered irritably. "Don't make any difference. The question is whether you got it or not."

"Yes, I've got it all but a few hundred dollars I used up in living."

"Where?"

Dex made a short, contemptuous laugh. "Like you said, Turnbull — what's the difference?"

The grey eyes held no especial menace in them. Dex was trying to imagine this hulk of man shooting a woman to death. It was hard to believe, if one judged John Turnbull by exterior appearances.

"Listen, Williams; I'm going to make you a proposition."

"Save your breath," Dex said curtly. "Your dad made me one, too. I wouldn't go along with you any more'n I'd go along with him."

"You won't turn it back to the company?"

"Sure. I've already told Will Herndon and Sheriff Bulow I'd do that."

"Well, what the hell's the hold-up, then? I'll have the charges dropped against you. My father's willing. You know that."

"I've got a damned good reason for keeping the money a while longer, Turnbull. I think you know what it is. The day I give over that money I'm a dead man, and you know it. I was damned near a dead man before, when that red-headed friend of yours tracked me down."

Turnbull's unblinking stare didn't waver. He leaned back a little so that he was half-sitting, half-leaning, against the table. "I'll do you better'n my father offered. I'll get the charges dropped and give you five hundred in cash to ride out of the country with. How's that sound?"

"Better," Dex said with a short nod.

"Then tell me where it's hid."

Dex ran a hand through his hair. It was long and shaggy. That surprised him, for he hadn't thought of a haircut in a long time. "Well, I don't know whether I could tell you exactly how to get there or not. I could find the place all right, but I'm not much of a hand at drawing maps and the like."

The grey eyes shone with a deep brightness. "That won't be hard to arrange," Turnbull said.

Slim Barr shoved off the wall. "John, if you've got any ideas about gettin' that money back by usin' Williams, you'll have to wait until Tom gets back. I can't authorise him to leave here, and I can't go with you."

Turnbull turned massively and regarded

Slim Barr with his vacant look. "Who the hell said you could? I know where Tom is. I know what he's after over there, too." He paused, and Dex, who was watching Barr's face, saw the sudden wash of disbelief go over the lawman's features. He followed the trajectory of Barr's downward glance and understood in a flash why the deputy was staring like that. Turnbull had a gun in his hand. It was pointing directly at the deputy's middle. The silence was weighty and thick before Turnbull spoke again. "This satisfy you, Barr?"

"Turnbull, you're crazy!"

It was a ridiculous thing to say, but Dex understood the lawman's amazement perfectly. Son of one of the wealthiest, most influential men in Lovell, John Turnbull was putting himself beyond the law. It was almost unbelievable.

"Not as crazy as you think," Turnbull said. "Move over there by Williams."

The deputy obeyed with shock, like frostbite, making his face pale and stiff-looking. Turnbull turned with him, and Dex saw the gun. It was cocked and steady, and very blue-looking. A new weapon. Brand, spanking new. Sardonically Dex thought there'd already been one shot fired out of it.

"Williams, take his gun and toss it under the bed. Now, Barr, you walk over here."

And Dex knew what that meant, too. So did Slim Barr. He hesitated, licked his lips and spoke words that were nearly whispered.

"Use a rope."

"Rope hell," Turnbull said dispassionately. "Get over here."

Dex watched as Barr crossed the room. His eyes were puckered against the blow they all knew was coming. When it came, Barr made no move to flinch, and Dex admired him for that; then he was staring down at the slumped, grotesquely-sprawled lawman, and Turnbull was standing wide-legged beside the table.

"Come on, Williams. I've got horses out front."

Dex stood up, thinking that Turnbull had it all thought out in advance. Must have had, if he had horses for their escape already tied outside and ready. He shrugged. "I can't walk too good, so take it slow."

Turnbull flicked him a long look, but said nothing. Neither of them were deceived, and both knew it. Turnbull would kill Dexter Williams the second he had the hidden money in his possession. If for no other reason than because he'd need the extra horse to pack it all away with him. Dex moved toward the door thinking Turnbull would look at it like that, too. It wouldn't matter that Dex, alive, would be a witness against him. That wasn't important to the icy-blooded man with the doleful look. What mattered was his escape with the money, and he'd need an extra horse to carry it.

Dex stopped at the door and shot back the bolt. "You'd better go first, Turnbull. If the road's clear, nod to me and I'll come out. Can't risk being seen going out of here, or there'll be half Lovell after us in a second."

Turnbull's unblinking stare held to Dex's face for a second, then he nodded and lumbered past Dex, holstered his gun and pulled back the door. If Williams still thought he was going to get five hundred dollars and a clean break, it might help them at that. He stood framed in the opening for a second, teetering on thick legs, then went a little farther outside and swung his head like an angry bear, looking up and down the roadway. Dex used the fleeting ten seconds to jump over beside Slim Barr, snatch up the lawman's gun and slide it into the waistband of his britches, in back, where his rumpled shirt would hide it — maybe.

"Let's go."

Dex opened the door and headed straight toward two saddled horses at the hitchrack. An experienced, fast look told him the animal with the longest stirrup leathers dangling along his sides would be Turnbull's horse. He went around to the near-side of the other beast, toed into the stirrup, jerked free the tie-rope and swung up. Turnbull nodded toward the south. They rode side by side with their backs towards the business section. Dex glanced once at the profile of his companion and looked away. There would be no expression there, even if Turnbull was as tense and tight inside as Dex was.

They went across the trash-littered lots and hit the range west of town. Dex remembered the last time he had ridden out of Lovell like that. With Slim Barr his prisoner; now things were reversed. He arched his back a little and felt the coldness of gunmetal. It made the perspiration run faster over his body. He had no doubts about his ability to out-gun John Turnbull under normal circumstances, but these weren't normal, not when the gun he carried was hidden underneath his baggy shirt and around in back at that.

"Now where?"

The smooth, well-fleshed face was turned toward him. He knew his mistake as soon as Turnbull spoke. He would have to lead the way. Turnbull would ride behind him. He would see the bulge of the gun under his shirt, back there.

"We can hold west like this for a long time yet."

"Did you cache it far out?"

"Yeah. About ten miles straight ahead, then north another ten or fifteen miles."

"Oh! Back in the trees?"

"Yeah." There was nothing for it but bluff. "Say, Turnbull, you don't happen to have an extra hip-holster in your pack, there, do you?"

The grey eyes showed a little mild interest. "No; why?"

Dex began awkwardly to fish out the gun from under his shirt. "I'm about rubbed raw from hiding this thing in my britches."

Turnbull looked at the gun stolidly, then lifted his glance to Dex's face. "The hell," he said in surprise. "You been hidin' that thing from the law?"

"Yeah."

"Well, I'll be damned. Didn't Tom strip you down?"

"Sure, but I managed to hide it out on him."

Something like a hard grin passed fleetingly over the heavy features. "Well, stick it in your britches in front. I've wore 'em that way. They don't rub like that."

And that was all John Turnbull said. Dex examined the gun and rammed it into the front of his pants behind the dented belt buckle. His eyes were contracted a little against the sun-smash that made the atmosphere dance, but the look in their depths was sly. It was the old foxfire that shone from the glance of all hunted men. John Turnbull didn't have it.

They rode in a steady line due west. The land lay as far as they went. There were odd, dark shadows cast before them by a clouding sky. The shadows moved east past them, little grey blotches that made it nearly impossible for them to be seen by the natural camouflage, and made it just as difficult for them to see a posse, should one be down-country from them. Dex rode in silence, feeling strong with the sun on his back in spite of the cloud shadows, and his mind was working ahead to the time when he knew there would be a showdown.

John Turnbull rode in dark silence. Dex could tell absolutely nothing from the man's face or bearing. Finally he turned northward, where a light growth of willows lined a little creek. Reaching from the saddle, he broke several of the willows and stripped a slim fingerling and put it thoughtlessly between his teeth.

"Turnbull, I heard you shot a woman last night. That true?"

"Who told you that?"

"Hell, several people. Seems like half Lovell knows about it."

"I did," Turnbull said coldly.

Dex watched the round, smooth face. It was

hard to tell, with the cloud-shadows running, but he thought a darker shade of red colour was in the big man's face.

"What about? Why'd you shoot her?"

That brought Turnbull's head around. His eyes were venomous. "Mind your own damned business, Williams."

"That's what I'm doing, feller," Dex said with equal hostility.

The grey eyes remained on Dex's face for moments before Turnbull spoke again. "What do you mean?"

"If you shot that woman, then you're running, Turnbull. You're not going back to Lovell. That means you'll take the money and keep on going."

"Well?"

"How about my record against the company? Who's going to get the charges dropped?"

Turnbull laughed. A short, unpleasant sound. "No one. You've got it figured right, Williams. I want that money to keep on going with. You'll get a cut of it. What the hell — you're an owlhoot; what do care about those charges against you? You've got something a darned sight more valuable. Your freedom. We'll both be free and foot-loose."

Dex said no more. There was no need to. Nor did he have any illusions about their sharing the money, either. He rode with a wary eye on young Turnbull, and chewed on the twig with a rhythmic, slow motion of his jaws.

When they hit the gradual slope that led up toward the purpling distance that was the forested uplands, Dex stopped on a high ridge, twisted in the saddle and looked back. The cloud-shadows made it hard to catch movement because the whole plain seemed to be moving.

"Nothin' back there. Come on."

Dex didn't move. There *was* something back there; had to be. He sat perfectly still watching. The sun was low and the shadows that didn't move were long and thin.

"What you waiting for?"

Dex turned and looked at the larger, younger man. "Looking for a posse. You didn't hit Barr hard enough for him to sleep this long."

"Expecting to see one, are you?"

Dex scorned the suspicious lilt of Turnbull's voice. "You're damned right I am. Two wanted murderers, Turnbull. The law won't sit back and pray for us to return. They'll come — you wait."

Turnbull swung his head and looked down the land with a cold, indifferent glance. "By the time they cut our sign we'll be so far away the devil couldn't find us."

"It won't be that easy," Dex said. "You're new at this hide-and-seek business. I'm not. When you've hid out as long as I have you'll know what I mean."

Turnbull shrugged and lifted his reins, held them aloft for a still second, then craned his neck a little, as though his eyes weren't too good at distances. Dex watched him, then swung to follow Turnbull's line of vision.

And it was movement all right, too. Small and distant, but movement coming toward them, against the billowy cloud-shadows that were moving eastward. The horsemen back there were coming westward. That made it easier to see them. Dex watched them without moving a muscle.

"Looks like a posse," John Turnbull said. "Don't know who else'd come up this way — do you?"

Dex wanted to smile at the sudden questioning way the big man put it. He slumped and fished for his tobacco sack. "No, it'd have to be a posse all right, and they're coming fast."

"Easy to track us now, too."

"Yeah. Easy as hell."

Turnbull swung to face him. There was anger in his face. "Don't be so damned sarcastic about it. They're after you as much as me."

Dex lit the cigarette and blew out smoke. "Don't worry, Turnbull. They won't get us."

"Why won't they?"

"Remember what I told you? I've been doing this for quite a spell. So far no posse's tracked me down. Doggoned hard to shag a man over pine needles, Turnbull. It can be done, but it's about the slowest work on earth."

Turnbull's face cleared a little. "That where you've got the company money hid out? In those damned trees?"

"Yeah. Let's go. I'd like to hit a camp I know of before dark."

They threw long, calculating looks back at the posse, then went on up the gradual slope until the first trees came out to meet them; then they passed in behind the bulwark of massive, fragrant trunks and high limbs overhead that made their world a dense place of soft shadows. They rode in among the stillness and gloom until evening came fully down upon them; then Dex swung out through the trees and led a fast pace toward their camp. He was smiling softly around the mouth, and he was dog-tired. His face was grey with fatigue, but the little grin hovered at the edges of his mouth, too. John Turnbull didn't see it, not even after Dex swung down on the west side of a little glade where the feed was almost knee-high to a mounted man, and waited for Turnbull to come up.

"This your camp?"

"One of 'em. Get down."

Turnbull did. Obeying without being aware that he had. He bent his heavy legs and made a face from the pain that went through him. He wasn't used to long rides. Dex was kicking needles off a little clump of firewood, picking up dry pieces for a fire. The big man watched him callously. Dex squatted near a firehole made of blackened rocks, and glanced up.

"Don't stand there, Turnbull. Get those horses unsaddled and hobbled."

That time Turnbull's eyes darkened. He caught the tone of the order as well as its brusqueness. "Who the hell you talking to, Williams?"

Dex arose very slowly. He was deadly tired, and ran his hands down the sides of his britches to get them steady, or at least hide their shakiness. "You," he said firmly. "You, Turnbull. Up here you'll get told what to do if you don't have sense enough to do it. Understand?"

Turnbull's grey eyes were like his father's blue eyes. Glacial cold and unfriendly. Dex watched him, waiting. They stood like stranger panthers eyeing each other, then Dex repeated himself with a slow softness.

"You understand?"

Turnbull very clearly was fighting with himself. It was a long and grim battle, too, for he didn't move until another full two minutes had elapsed; then, very suddenly, he dropped his reins and turned to unsaddle his horse. Dex had won. He squatted and lit the little fire with that same secretive smile around his mouth, but the rest of his face was blank and hard-looking. His idea of making Turnbull do the fighting from now on had weathered its first test. He meant to humble the stage line owner's son. Humble and break him, then show him the gold, because he was taking him to it, but by a slow and indirect route. Let him see it . . .

"Williams; they might see that damned fire."

"You're pretty green, Turnbull. My hat'd cover this fire. The glare won't rise up ten feet. This is a cooking fire, not a signal fire. Let's have your pack there. You got food in it?"

Turnbull didn't answer, but he passed over the pack. There was food in it. Enough to last one man quite a while and two men not so long. Dex laughed in a thin, rasping way.

"More'n enough grub in here."

"It's got to last, remember that."

"Sure," Dex said, smiling peculiarly at

Turnbull. "It'll last as long as either one of us want it."

"What d'you mean by that? Listen, Williams —" The threat that started was bitten off right there.

"Rope it and eat."

No more was said until they had eaten, cleaned up the camp and Dex re-packed the food and utensils. Then Turnbull refused Dex's tobacco sack and leaned back against a tree trunk watching the shorter man smoke.

"Bein' a free man sure changed you, Williams."

Dex looked into the still, grey eyes. "No, it wasn't that that did it. It was the way I got free, Turnbull."

"You mean about me takin' you out?"

"Yeah. Only you didn't do it voluntarily."

"The hell I didn't. If my gun didn't do it, what did?"

"Marge Herndon."

Dex let it lie there in the silence that grew between them. Very slowly John Turnbull gathered in his bulk and straightened off the tree trunk. His eyes had wonder and suspicion in them. "Explain what you mean, Williams," he said evenly.

"Before you came to the sheriff's office, you met Marge on the walk outside your place, didn't you?"

But the big man's appearance of stolidness was belied when he answered. His mind had worked rapidly ahead. He had guessed it before Dex told him. "So you put her up to that? That was pretty clever, Williams. Why?"

"Because I knew if your dad hadn't already told you I had the money and had it cached away, then Marge would tell you. I asked her to. Wrote her a note saying for her to hunt you up and tell you I could be persuaded to turn it over to you in exchange for my freedom."

"Go on." Turnbull's lips were pursed.

"She told you, and you know the rest. You came up to see me — and here we are."

"You used me to get you out of jail?"

Dex nodded. "That's right."

Turnbull considered it thoughtfully for a moment, then leaned back against the tree again. "Why?" he asked. "You had a gun."

"But they watched me too closely. You could get in and they'd trust you."

"All right; how'd you know I'd gun you out of there?"

"I wasn't sure, but I had an idea that if you really did kill that girl over at the Flats, and they didn't have enough proof on you to lock you up yet, that maybe I could provide you with a good reason for lighting out. If Tom had come back with blood in his eye

177

he'd of arrested you. You knew whether he'd come after you or not. I didn't. When you came to the office I knew you'd killed her. The only reason you'd face me would be to get that money and use it to run with. You came and gunned me out of Bulow's office. That meant you'd killed her all right."

Turnbull was almost smiling. It added nothing especially to his heavy, ponderous features. "You're no damned fool, Williams," he said. "You used me."

"Yeah; just like you used me."

"How? What makes you think I used you?"

"Cut it out, Turnbull. I'm not trying to kid you, and you're not going to horse me around. For one thing, how'd that red-headed hombre happen to be trackin' me?"

"Bauman, or whatever his name was?" Turnbull shrugged. "He was after the company's reward money, as far as I know."

"I told you," Dex said, "you aren't going to horse me around. If you don't tell me why he was after my scalp, then I'll tell you."

"All right; you tell me, then."

"Because you hired him to run me down and leave my carcass in some drygulch somewhere."

Turnbull regarded Dex with a pensive glance. "That's right. Know the rest of it?"

"I can guess, but I've done enough talking.

178

You tell *me* now."

"Sure. The company's reward wasn't enough to get him to take your trail, so I doubled it. He was to bring me back your gun and wallet so's I'd know he got you."

"Why?"

"Why?" Turnbull said slowly. "Because you caused the company a hell of a lot of grief."

Dex snorted derisively. "We're alone now, Turnbull. You can quit lying."

But Turnbull didn't speak again. He sat there looking at Dex like he was appraising a person he'd badly misjudged.

"All right. Tell me why you killed the dance-hall girl."

"She wasn't a dance-hall girl, damn you!"

Dex was startled by the barely-restrained fury in the man's voice. He shifted his approach quickly with an apologetic shrug. "Well, whoever she was, why'd you kill her?"

"Because I had to."

"That doesn't say much. What's the rest of it? Listen, Turnbull; we're head over heels in this murder business together. I've spilt what I know. You'd better do the same."

"I had to kill her," Turnbull repeated. His grey eyes were damp and anguished in the pale gloom that was held a few feet away by the dying embers of the little cooking-fire. "I — she — she — had been getting money from me for almost a year. We were going to get a ranch down in Mexico. Go there and live. But she didn't keep the money like she was supposed to."

"All right," Dex said quietly, "that's enough."

"The hell is it," Turnbull flared at him, as though he had interrupted a bitter-sweet reverie without an excuse. "She gave the money to a man I thought was her brother."

"And he wasn't her brother. Her lover, maybe?"

"Lover? No; he was her husband. He took the money, and when I went over there last night — we had a little adobe place out of town where we met — she was — was —"

"Yeah," Dex said, at a loss for words but wanting the larger man to stop talking about it. "I know. She was with her husband, and you walked in." Turnbull nodded. "How'd you miss the husband?"

"I didn't shoot at him, and by the time I would've, he'd run out of the damned place and I couldn't find him."

"And he turned you in to the law?"

"It had to be him, Williams. No one else knew about our hideaway."

"I wouldn't bet on that," Dex said cynically.

"Folks have a way of smelling things like that. But why the devil didn't you just up and marry her? I mean, why didn't you ask her to marry you before you found out about this brother-husband hombre?"

"I did. I asked her a dozen times. First off, though, my father refused to allow it. Later, when I told her I'd cut loose from the old man, she said we shouldn't do that until we had the money for our ranch."

Dex scooped up some handfuls of dirt and tossed them on the little fire. He hated the man across the fire from him, but he didn't like looking at his tortured, naked soul, either. They sat in the fragrant gloom until the moon came up, then Dex got up and stretched. His body felt weak but able; then he let his arms sag and looked over at the unmoving bulk of man against the tree trunk.

"Come on, Turnbull. Time to ride."

The grey eyes lifted, sought Dexter's face and stayed there. "You worrying about that posse?" It was the old John Turnbull. If he had been shaken before, it was either over with or hidden behind the smooth, round mask of his face now.

"Not afraid of it; just don't want to let it catch up to us. Get up. Let's go. Fetch the horses while I get things ready."

Turnbull arose, brushed the pine needles

181

off himself methodically, and turned out into the little meadow where the hobbled animals were standing, full and listless, drowsing.

Dex stopped working when the big man's back was to him. He watched Turnbull amble after their mounts, and there was a strange sheen of triumph in the look on his face. It was almost an impersonal look of victory, but it hadn't abated by the time Turnbull came back and handed Dex his tie-rope, then bent to pick up his saddle.

Dex led out. He didn't like riding in front of the killer, but he felt reasonably safe. Would feel that way at least until they got to the cache and had dug it up. After that he knew, as well as John Turnbull knew, what would happen to Dexter Williams if he wasn't on his toes.

They rode through the long hours of the chilly night. Fall was coming. It had little winter-streamers laying the groundwork in its advance. They were laced through the cool upland atmosphere like unseen icicles. The riders felt them whenever they rode into a low spot, or down across a narrow canyon. Cold air that lay down in those places waiting to chill them.

And the night was long. The forest was a haunted place after midnight. Once a cougar cried out in its coughing, falsetto scream.

Dex's horse bunched under him. He reached down with his right hand and took a handful of mane hair and twisted it gently, to get the animal's mind off bucking. It worked, as it usually does, and Dex relaxed again. In his present shape, he knew any horse under the sun could unload him easily. The strength in his body was marginal stuff. Sufficient for average use, it wasn't up to supplying the vice-strength and quick equilibrium he'd need to ride a bucking horse among tall trees with hard, scaly trunks that could, and would, break a man's back like matchwood.

There was a doubtful kind of satisfaction in knowing that John Turnbull was tiring, too. It came to Dex when the renegade spoke through chattering teeth as they made their way up out of a deep arroyo, using narrow and twisting game trails.

"Dammit all, Williams, let's stop and get warm for a while. That posse can't find us in here anyway."

"Maybe not, but I'd rather not chance it. It isn't much farther before we hit another bivouac spot."

That was all Dex would say in spite of repeated protestations from young Turnbull. And Dex knew, as Turnbull did also, that for the time being Dexter Williams, not the treacherous man behind him, had the whip-

183

hand. If they became separated, the loot would still belong to Williams, and John Turnbull would be worse than broke — he would also be hopelessly lost in a maze of large, silent trees and mysterious folds of hills that rolled endlessly westward as far as they could see.

It was clever. So clever that the wily Turnbull didn't understand just how completely Dex had foxed him. Turned the tables so that he was more than dependant on Dexter Williams. He was totally and irredeemably lost without him. Lost in the forest; lost to his goal, the hidden money cache, and lost in his desperate need to escape the lawmen who were somewhere far behind them, floundering and cursing their way through the trees, praying for sunup to come and let them see the tracks they needed to follow the desperados by.

"I thought you said it was only about ten or twelve miles to your cache from that last camp?"

Dex twisted in his saddle, shot Turnbull an annoyed glance, then swung forward again. "I'm a poor judge of distance. Always went more by time than miles. We'll have to stop a little ways up here and wait for daylight, but I want to be close enough so's we'll have a good start after we dig it up. Plenty of daylight to ride away in. Never did care for this

184

night-riding. Especially among these damned trees. Feller never can tell when he's going to get knocked out of the saddle by a low limb."

Turnbull grunted and swore. "You sure you aren't lost?"

"I don't think so," Dex said laconically; then, through the fringe of trees ahead he saw a white, ghostly-looking clearing and made for it. "No; I recognise this place all right. We'll rest here until sunup."

Turnbull rode through the last fringe of trees and ducked his head to avoid a low limb, then he reined up and looked around at the little park. "This another of your damned camps?" he asked sullenly.

Dex was down, stretching his legs. "Nope," he said, almost cheerily, "but it's far enough inland so's the lawmen won't get near it before noon to-morrow. By then we ought to be riding separate ways with enough money to last us both a long time."

Turnbull got down stiffly and began to unsaddle his horse. His voice came muffled. "How much's in the cache?"

Dex flung his saddle down, hobbled and slipped off the bridle. "You ought to know that better'n I do."

"Well, I know how much you took, but I don't know how much you spent."

Dex straightened up, looking hard at Turnbull's back. "I spent around five hundred or so for living. Grub and the like. Deduct that, and the six thousand you robbed up at Mesilla, and you'll have the answer on how much is left in the cache."

Turnbull turned slowly, dumped his saddle and regarded Dex blankly. "What made you say that?"

"About Mesilla? Well, *I* didn't get it. You're the only other feller robbing the Green Springs company, so you must've taken it. Didn't you? Hell, if *you* didn't, there's someone else running a hot iron on us."

Turnbull turned back to his horse, took the hobbles off his saddle, knelt and put them around the animal's front pasterns without speaking. Dex was watching him. He wanted to grin, but he didn't. Turnbull got up and slipped off the bridle, and tossed it carelessly on top of his saddle and saddle-blanket, then he slouched and watched Dex making a cigarette. The shorter, older man held up the sack.

"Smoke?"

"No; don't use 'em."

Dex lay down facing Turnbull. There was an amused glint in his eyes. The big man towered over him, impassive and sturdy and uneasy-looking.

"Well?" Dex said.

Turnbull inclined his head a little, reluctantly. "Yeah, I robbed the Mesilla office."

"I knew that. Figured it, anyway; but how the devil did you do it? That's quite a ride from Lovell."

Turnbull sat down and leaned back on his saddle. "It's a long way, but you can make it damned fast and be back in time for supper if you just figure ahead a little."

"How?"

"Relay, Williams. I took four horses out and hid 'em along the way in the trees and canebreaks the day before. Then I got an early start and fanned the breeze, got into Mesilla after dark, when I figured no one'd recognise me, and walked into our office up there with my key. When I'd opened the safe, I took the money and rode back the same way. After I used up each horse, I just turned 'em loose. They came drifting back to the company's pasture at the edge of town the following day, and I rode out there and let 'em back in the gate."

"I'll be damned," Dex said softly. "You know, Turnbull, you're no fool."

The big man laughed. It was a harsh sound, and ironic. "Yes, I am. The biggest goddamned fool in the world."

Dex let it go at that. He stared up into the

trees and didn't altogether agree with his enemy. He had been a fool over a woman, yes, but he'd been dangerously clever in almost everything else. Well, Dex wanted to work him like he'd worked Dex, and he was doing it, too, but he was walking a mighty thin trail. Turnbull was no fool. One slip and Dexter Williams was a dead man. But it wouldn't happen yet. Not for another day, at least, and in the meantime he was dog-tired. He was moving his hips, making hollows in the pine needles and getting ready to sleep, when Turnbull rolled slightly and faced him.

"Tell me something, Williams. Where'd Herndon get that six thousand dollars he shipped? A man can work a saddle shop all his damned life and not save up that much."

"I don't know," Dex lied, but the jolt of the question made him wrench around and eye the big man cautiously, suspiciously. Turnbull was no fool, and Dex wanted to know what had prompted that remark. "Why?"

"I've been thinking. If he had that much, maybe he's got more."

"Oh!" Relief flooded through Dex like ecstasy; then he smiled thinly. "You thinking of taking up the owlhoot business for a profession? Because if you are, let me tell you something. It isn't worth the grief. You may make a few good hauls, but you'll sleep on hard ground most of your life, and you'll never be able to relax or trust anyone — I know."

Turnbull cleared his throat, spat, and coughed. "I reckon," he said. "Anyway, Lovell's too hot for me for a while. But there's something else, too. That six thousand was in new money. Looked like it came out of an express box. I've been wondering about that ever since I got it. You reckon Herndon's robbing the company, too?"

Dex was sweating. He faked a wondering, long pause, then wrinkled his head. "The way you say it, it sounds like he might be at that."

"Well — there's a way to tell . . ." John Turnbull's voice trailed off suddenly. Dex reached down and gripped the six-gun with a cold hand and waited. Very slowly the big man sat up, turned and faced him. His eyes were wide. "Williams — you said — back there — I just caught it. The cache you've got of company money — it's short the five hundred or so you've used up, plus the six thousand I stole from Mesilla."

Dexter nodded gently. "That's right. I've been waiting for you to remember that, Turnbull. That six thousand was planted there. I gave it to Will Herndon to ship up there. I had him deliver it to you personally, at the Lovell office, and get a receipt for it.

He did. You didn't have to tell me how you got up there and robbed the safe. I had no idea *how* you did it, but I knew *that* you did it."

"Herndon planted it," Turnbull repeated slowly.

"Yeah, that's why the cache is short six thousand more'n I spent."

"You — suspected me, Williams, didn't you?"

"Hell yes. Right from the day that first stage was held up."

"How?"

Dexter made a wry face. "A man as smart as you are, Turnbull, ought to be able to figure that out easy enough. That red-headed hombre you call Bauman. He identified me right off. Of course, it might've been mistaken identity. I thought it was until I remembered how you told Sheriff Bulow about yelling and that the safe was crowbarred that first time Green Springs company was robbed. You were lying. No one knew it but me, Turnbull. I knew it because I was in the next room and would have heard any noise like that — if there had been any. There wasn't, so that meant you told the law that so's they think *I* was lying when I said I didn't hear any noise. That was the truth, but they didn't believe me. After all, I'm an ex-convict and you're the son of a big man in Lovell."

"You've known right along, then."

"Hell, yes. You're smart all right, Turnbull, but you're not the smartest man around. My trouble was that I couldn't make anyone believe me."

"But you went out and turned renegade after that," Turnbull said accusingly.

"Sure I did. There wasn't anything else for me to do. But there's a limit to what I'll do, too. That's not true in your case. I wouldn't shoot a stranger down in cold blood to frame an innocent man. I wouldn't have used a carbine to create the effect that I was an ex-convict and didn't own a pistol. And I wouldn't have hired that red-headed gunman to hunt me down, kill me in cold blood if he could, and get the law satisfied that the highwayman and murderer was dead, so's they drop the investigation — all so's you and some lousy wench in Mex town could run away with your old man's money." Dex's face was flushed with black anger. "I wouldn't have done half the things you did, feller, not for the best girl or the most money in the damned world."

Turnbull was rigid. His face was white, but its impassiveness hadn't altered a bit. If anything, it was more stony and unreadable than ever. All he said was: "So you knew all the time."

"About the robberies, sure. About the reason, no."

The silence descended between them again. It lasted a long time, but Turnbull broke it finally. "And now what?"

"The cache, remember?"

The grey eyes tried to look beyond Dex's flinty stare; then Turnbull slumped, hugged his knees with powerful arms, and rocked back and forth. "You're still an outlaw."

"The outlaw you made me. I didn't kill that passenger — you did. I didn't rob that safe the first time, either. That was you again. You used me right from the start. Made me an outlaw. Well, now it's your turn."

"How do you mean, my turn?"

"First, reach down with your left hand and toss that gun away, then I'll tell you."

"And if I don't?"

"The magpies'll be picking your eyes out by sunup. That answer you?"

Turnbull reached down and threw his pistol aside. His motions were deliberate and careful, but his eyes were hooded with a savageness Dex hadn't seen in them before. He guessed — correctly — that it was the man's killer look. The craftiness and rancour and cold-bloodedness all combined, but when Turnbull raised his head and looked at Dex again, head-on, his face was as blank as ever.

"How much of the loot do I get?"

It surprised Dex; then he remembered that Turnbull thought he was still on the dodge, too, which he was, but not if Marge had done the other thing he'd written in that note. Not, that is, if more than planning and incredible luck, and a few other things, happened to be in his favour — for once.

"Where would you go?"

Turnbull shrugged. "Just go," he said. "Just light out and keep going. What's the difference?"

Dex didn't answer him. He felt no pity for the man, only a vast wonder that anyone would have such a warp to their character as to willingly get themselves into the spot John Turnbull was in. He arose, went over where Turnbull's gun was, picked it up, emptied the cylinder, and pointed the thing at Turnbull's middle. "Shuck that shell-belt and holster. I'll need 'em more'n you will."

After Turnbull had complied, and Dex had encircled his waist with the cartridge belt and slid his own gun into the flapping holster, he sat down again, swung his arm in a mighty heave and sent Turnbull's empty gun sailing into the night.

"Who was that hombre you shot to death on the coach? You know?"

Turnbull shook his head. "No," he said, "I

don't know. Had it figured out that if folks got mad enough about that killing, when they thought you were the killer, they might lynch you."

"You wanted me put away fast, didn't you? First try and get me strung up for a murder you did, then you sent that red-headed gunman to knock me off."

"Yeah," Turnbull said in his inflectionless voice. "I had to get rid of you fast, Williams. Otherwise the damned law might stumble onto something. You can't tell; they're thickheaded and all, but a man can't think of everything, when he's busy like I was."

"No," Dex said dryly, "I reckon not. Even your dad was out to string me up. You came within an ace of winning at that, Turnbull. It was closer'n I ever want to come again."

"All right; you know the whole story. Know as much as I do, now, and it's all behind us. Now — what's ahead?"

Dex laughed bitterly. "Just like that. You damned near get me killed, and you sure as the devil have got me outlawed from hip to shoulder, and just like that we're going to forget all about it and talk about what's next. Well, go right on guessing, Turnbull. You've had your licks, now I'm having mine."

When Dex looked away from the big man's shadowed face he could see the sun lightening up the eastern sky through the treetops. It was a grey, unhealthy-looking pastel shade that carried no warmth and little cheer.

"Get up, Turnbull. Go get the horses. We've still got a little ride ahead of us."

They went out of the little park with Turnbull in the lead and Dex directing him. Both of them were beard-stubbled, dirty and unkempt-looking. Both were renegades . . .

Chapter Six

They were riding when the sun was above the horizon, and they were still astride when it was nearly overhead. Twice Dex gave Turnbull terse directions. Once the big man turned in the saddle and looked back at Dex with a cold, hostile look.

"You know where the hell you are, Williams?"

"What's the difference?" Dex said, mimicking his companion. "You're still a free man."

The grey eyes showed a flash of venom; then they rode on again, and before noon they were beginning to travel downhill a little. A gradual, gentle sloping that let them see open country in brief flashes through the trees. After that, for some inexplicable reason, Turnbull seemed satisfied. It was as though the trees at their densest had oppressed him, and well they might, for his house of cards had collapsed back there in the forest, and the man he had fully intended to rob and kill when they got to Dex's cache, was his captor instead of his captive. Not that

196

Dex said so; he didn't.

The sun was hot in the clearings, but far off they could see the trees turning colour a little. Not the firs and pines and evergreens, but the cottonwoods and locusts and other trees that shed a golden, leafy treasure every fall. There was beauty, but neither of the horsemen saw it then.

"See that trail on your right, over there? The one that leads off between those two birches? Well, take it north."

"What the hell is 'north'?"

"To your right," Dex said; then he wagged his head a little. "Turnbull, you wouldn't have lasted a week on the backtrails. You're smart — no one's going to deny that — but you're dumb as hell in the things that count, on the owlhoot trail."

"I wasn't goin' In'yun, Williams."

"That's good, because you'd of died in the back country."

They went another four or five miles, then Dex called out to Turnbull to stop on a sere, lonely ledge ahead of them. He did, scanning the country around as though he had no idea where he was, which was the case. Dex rode up nearby and stood in his stirrups. He was staring with a hard-eyed intensity into a long, narrow defile that lay below them like a monstrous snake, winding through the mountains until it debouched upon some distant, unseen prairie, the dry passageway of some long extinct river. There was a wealth of violent colour down there where the trees grew on either side of the defunct streambed. If there was movement down there, Dex didn't see it.

He frowned, lost in thought, then he shrugged and spoke, pointing with his left hand and arm, and didn't look at John Turnbull.

"See that trail that winds down yonder? The one over by that pine with the lightning-struck trunk?"

Turnbull followed Dex's point, saw the blackened, dying carcass of the pine tree. "Yeah. We go down there?"

"Right as rain, Turnbull. Hit that trail and keep going. I'll tell you when to haul up."

Turnbull reined his horse toward the trail and spoke without looking back. The words came over the slip-stream of his massive shoulder. "Your cache down there in that old creek-bed?"

"Yeah."

They went over the twisting, turning trail through a world that gradually changed from the sombre sameness of the evergreens to the flamboyant multicoloured shade of the trees that would soon drop their yellow, purple, red and black leaves. Down around the lip of shale and mulch that was trodden deep, like an old scar, against the cheek of the big hill they were descending, and finally they came out in the creek-bed and Turnbull pulled up, twisted in his saddle and regarded Dex owlishly.

"Now where?"

"Straight ahead until you come to a big old oak with a cottonwood sapling next to it, bent over and weighted to the ground with rocks."

"And that's it?"

Dex's eyes swung to the big man's face. He nodded. "That's it."

Turnbull didn't move. Dex, watching him, had an uneasy feeling. "Well?" he said. "You want me to lead you?"

"No, not 'specially. I want you to tell me something, though."

"What?"

"What's going to happen to us after we get down there and find your cache?"

"The best way to find that out," Dex said, "would be to ride on down there."

"There's no reward on me, Williams," Turnbull said in his level voice. "You wouldn't get a dime off my carcass. You know that, don't you?"

Dex's triumph was almost complete. He smiled acidly. "Wasn't counting on any, but

I wouldn't bet there won't be one by now, either."

"You can't collect it without giving yourself up."

Dex's face darkened a little; what glints of hard humour might have been in his eyes, were dormant now. "I'm not interested in bounty money, Turnbull. I'm not interested in you at all, except as a means of getting out of trouble. Now turn around and ride on down toward that tree with the rocks on it, or I'll leave you right here, and not on a horse, either."

Turnbull's cold glance lingered a second, then fell away from Dex's face only to return a moment later. "You'd shoot a man in the back," he said with no great emotion in the words.

Dex snorted. "You figure other fellers by yourself, don't you? Turnbull, that's exactly what you had in mind for me, when we rode out of Lovell. Get me to lead you to the cache, get the money, then leave me lying there. Your kind's no mystery to me, Turnbull, but I don't work the same way. I'm not going to kill you."

"Then why," Turnbull asked with a puzzled squint, "are you taking me to the cache? I thought for a while you were just leading me around through the hills on a wild goose chase. I still think you were stalling most of the time, because when we were on that ledge up there I could see the Flats where we came up out of Lovell. We've been riding in a hell of a big circle."

Dex nodded brusquely. "That's right; I've been stalling for time with you, but I'm not doing it any more."

"Why did you do it? Killing time until you could get the drop on me; was that it?"

"Partly," Dex admitted, "but not altogether that. You'll find out directly."

But Turnbull persisted. He was frankly and obviously bewildered, and showed it in his glance. "Well, why're you taking me to the cache? Do you figure to give me enough to get out of the country, or what?"

Dex leaned on his saddle-horn and fixed the larger man with a hard look. "Listen, Turnbull; I could be taking you to the loot because I want to see you sweat when you have to do the digging, but that's not it, either. You can't guess why I'm taking you where the money is at all, and I want it that way. Like I told you last night, you used me and now I'm using you. Call it a man's pride if you want to. No one likes to be made a horse's rear-end, and I'm no exception. You outsmarted me right down the line. Now I'm proving to myself that I'm just as smart as you are. That satisfy you?"

"Maybe," the big man said, "but you're sure not helping either of us get farther away from Lovell while you're horsing around playing king-bee. You know that, don't you?"

"What're you worrying about?" Dex demanded. "Tom Bulow's at least half-a-day behind us. Eb Bulow's up in Mesilla, or was until last night, and you left Slim Barr knocked out, so he's out of the running. Even if that's his posse on our back-trail, we've got nothing to fear from 'em. They won't find us unless we want them to."

Turnbull's puzzlement was increased by Dex's facts, rather than appeased. He shook his head in bewilderment. "For a while, though, I thought you were playing Will Herndon into the chase some way. He's the only one I can't account for. The others I know are out of the race."

"You can quit worrying about Will, if you want to. He went up to Mesilla, too, about the same time young Bulow did."

"There's only that posse we saw, then. All right; what the hell's this amount to, this stalling?"

Dex lifted his reins and nodded his head. "Ride on down to the cache and you'll find out."

They sat staring at one another for a full

minute before John Turnbull let his breath come out in an audible rush, swung forward in the saddle and booted his horse out down the creek-bed.

They rode the last half-a-mile in absolute silence; then, somewhere up ahead, a blue-jay began his raucous, excited screeching. Dex was tense and erect in the saddle. His hand rested lightly on the walnut butt of the gun he wore, and his face was pinched tight with apprehension.

Turnbull stopped his horse, dropped his big hands to the saddle-horn, and sat staring at a little sapling that was bent double, the leafy top hidden beneath a burden of carefully-piled rocks. It looked like an old Indian blaze. Dex rode up close behind the stopped horse and flashed his eyes over the banked-up clutches of trees on both sides of them. His heart was beating with a steady, increased thunder that echoed through his body.

"Get down, Turnbull. Go over where that bent tree is, pull off the rocks, and start digging."

Turnbull's eyes were bright and treacherous-looking. "With what?" he asked.

"Your damned hands! That's what I used — you can use yours, too."

Turnbull swung down stiffly and flexed his legs. He shot a hard look up at the hillside they had descended, then flung a careless glance at the canyon around them, dropped his reins and went forward, and, kneeling by the bent tree, began to pull the rocks aside. He worked feverishly until the back of his shirt was dark with sweat; then he straightened up, flung water off his face, and looked over his shoulder at Dex.

"How deep'd you bury the stuff, anyway?"

"Just dig," Dex said curtly, "and, say — are you sure your old man wouldn't have let you marry that dance-hall girl?"

The grey eyes clouded with resentment. "I told you he wouldn't, didn't I?"

"Yeah, but what the hell," Dex said, "robbing your own company over a woman — that's pretty raw, isn't it?"

Goaded, the big man glared savagely up at Dex, who was lounging in his saddle with a peculiar smile around his mouth. A wolf might wear such a smile before he brought down an unsuspecting doe.

"Listen, Williams; if you knew my father like I do, you wouldn't worry about robbing the old cuss. He threatened to run me out of the country if I had anything to do with her. That's why we had to rig up a secret meeting-place over at the Flats. That's why I wanted to break the old devil before I went down into Mexico. Show him I wasn't a weakling. Break that damned stage company he thought so much of. Hell, that's all life's been to him since my mother died. Green Springs Stage and Transfer Company. Why, the damned old scoundrel — he wouldn't even give me a share in the business until I'd worked three years as a manager for him."

Dex was nodding his head. The odd light that shone out of his eyes was granite hard and bright-looking. "That's better'n you deserve, Turnbull. He should've started making a man out of you ten years ago. Maybe you'd of got some iron in your backbone if he had. Instead, you shot and killed a perfect stranger in a Green Springs stage just to frame me. You robbed the company's safe in Lovell and framed me again. Then you robbed up in Mesilla, hired a gunman to drygulch me, and wound it all up by killing the woman you were stealing your old man into bankruptcy over. You're quite a feller, Turnbull, aren't you?"

The big man's face was stained with hatred. It showed through the oily sweat and out of the grey, lifeless eyes with their overcast of cold-bloodedness. He swore at Dex, spitting out the words like they were bullets. Biting them off in fierce rage that was closer to violent rebellion against Dex's position and six-gun than Dex knew.

When the savagery died away, Dex hadn't moved from his bent-over study of the kneeling man. Very slowly he shook his head. "Feel better now?" The unruffled supremacy of the shorter man was like armour. Turnbull felt it, saw and knew that he couldn't shake the other man's confidence; and that, more than anything else, was what broke his resistance. He sagged, looked down at the hole in front of him, and went back to work. His words came back to Dex lacking intonation. The man on the horse listened without blinking, without moving, in fact, but still wearing his little harsh grin of triumph.

"All right; maybe I didn't have the old man's guts, but I've got more brains than he's ever had. Rob him? Goddammit, Williams, I'd of killed him if I could. He made me earn what I got. What the hell was the sense of it? He's got money; always has had it. What's the sense in not spending it if you got it? Well, I came within an ace of breaking him; that's my revenge. If you hadn't been smarter than I figured you were, I'd of had his money, too, before long. I'd of robbed him blind, then broke his damned company, too. It meant more'n getting that ranch in Mexico. It meant getting my revenge, too. I'm still not sorry. About the girl, yes. About my father, no. I'd do it again if I got the chance. If I ever get the chance, I'll still do it. I'll kill him some-day."

"You will, you dirty, rotten whelp? You will?"

Dex's hand flashed to his hip. The explosion that came next was so sudden young Turnbull leapt erect like his legs were powerful springs. His eyes bulged, and the impassiveness was gone.

"Dad!"

Old man Turnbull was bent over, swearing in an awful monotone, and holding the arm Dex's bullet had shattered. His six-gun was lying in the rocks of the creek-bed where it had been knocked by the impact of Dex's bullet and the old man's violent reaction to the shot. John Turnbull swung slowly, like he was drugged, and glared at Dex. He met a flat, flinty stare above the tendril of dirty grey smog that wound up from the gun Dex was holding.

"Williams — you did this? You — knew he — was here — in those trees?"

Dex nodded, saying nothing, fascinated by the terrible look of shock and disbelief that was in the killer's grey, lifeless eyes.

"That was it. That was why you stalled. That was why you kept me going around in circles. It wasn't Will Herndon or the Bulows or the law you wanted to catch me — it was my father. You son of a — !"

"Rope it, John."

Dex shifted his glance to the newcomer who stepped out of the trees, and recognised the burly, squat man as Lovell's blacksmith.

"You bad hurt, Mister Turnbull?"

The old man had a tight grip on his wounded arm. A little, dark scarlet trickle oozed past his claw-like fingers. He was looking past his son, staring hard at Dex when he answered the blacksmith. "Hurt?" he said, in that reedy, rasping, unpleasant voice of his. "Hurt? Why, goddamn you, Mike, I've had more of these in my time than you've ever seen. Fetch a rag and bind it off, Mike," he went on. "Tight, mind you. Goddamned tight."

The blacksmith holstered his gun and moved closer to the old man. He tugged a dark blue handkerchief out of a hip pocket and went to work.

Frederick Turnbull hadn't taken his eyes off Dex Williams. He was ignoring his son as though he didn't exist. "You run a hell of a risk, Williams. I don't mind telling you, I'd of killed you. I'd of gut-shot you when you came out'n those goddamned trees if Mike hadn't stopped me. Why'd you do it? You could've told me some other way."

Dex made a sardonic smile. "The hell I

could've," he said bluntly. "Call the rest of 'em out of the trees, Turnbull. How many'd you fetch with you?"

"Come out, boys," the old man called out in his rasping voice. "Come out where Mister Williams can see you." He waited. Dex watched them emerge from cover. Three more, unfamiliar faces, walked into the creek-bed and stood there looking from the old man to Dex, where he still sat on his horse. Dex swung back to face the old man.

"They Green Springs company men?"

"Sure. Company men make the best hangrope possemen I know of."

"So they tell me," Dex said dryly. "I'm glad you believed Marge. If you hadn't, I'd of had a little harder time of it. I'd of brought him to your house in town and made him tell you all of it — and that wouldn't have been easy."

The blacksmith finished his crude but effective bandaging, and the iron-hearted old man grinned fiercely, showing stained snags of old teeth. "We're even, Williams. Bullet for bullet. Why'd you do it — save him, I mean?"

"Because I can't see much sense in a man killin' his own son."

"He deserves it. You heard what he said, didn't you?"

Dex looked scornfully at Frederick Turnbull. "Listen, you old scarecrow, you tried to make a man out of a feller that didn't have it in him to *be* a man. So, instead of a man, you made a killer. You're as much at fault as he is. You heard what he said about your damned company, didn't you? That it was all you lived for. Well, I believe him. I've heard stories about you, and I wish I'd been around when you were young and tough. I'd of tied a goddamned knot in your tail for you."

The elder Turnbull was hot-eyed, and his face was clouding over with black thunderclouds of anger. Dex noted it and ignored it. He swung down off his horse and walked over in front of the old man, stopped and gave him glare for glare.

"I think your son's a no-good son of a gun. I also think you helped to make him that way. He's caused me a lot of grief, and came damned close to gettin' me killed. So'd you — you and your damned hangrope justice. Turnbull, if you were thirty years younger I'd beat you half to death, then make you crawl the length of Lovell's main road eatin' dust! But it's too late for that, so I'm going to do something else, you damned old buzzard."

"What?" The old man's mouth hung slightly agape. He wasn't as wildly angry as he had been. Instead he was shocked and shaken. He had brought the four men with him to the spot Marge had given him the map of. Dex had drawn it for her on that paper he'd given her. Now here they were, standing in stunned amazement. No one had ever, in any of their recollections, talked like that to either of the Turnbulls before.

"I'm going to make you pay for the suffering you've caused me."

"How?"

"How?" Dex said bitterly. "Why, in about the only way a darned old devil like you can be hurt — right in your purse." He stepped back and nodded harshly toward the hole where John Turnbull had dug and exposed the first layer of sacking over the money hidden there.

"By getting a receipt from you for exactly one-half the loot that's in that hole, that's how."

The heavily-muscled blacksmith growled deep in his throat, like a warning dog might. Dex turned his head a little and faced him. His eyes were bright with killing anger. "You keep out of this, feller. Plenty of time for you boys to go into action after the old man makes up his mind, if he's got one to make up." He faced Turnbull again. "Spit or close the window," he said. "Your draw, you old devil — draw or drop out!"

Turnbull senior was standing there, for all the world like an emaciated and antiquated buzzard, lean to the point of skeletal thinness, watery-eyed, but icy-eyed, too. He ignored all of them but the scuffed, grey-looking face of the stocky-built man in front of him; then, very strangely, he smiled, showing the brown, scraggy old teeth again.

"By God, Williams, you're a horse trader. All right, I'm not scairt o' you for a second. I'll tell you that right now. Shoot and be damned to you. You nor any man livin' can make me do anything. But you win this hand. I'll take your deal on one condition."

"What?" Dex said coldly. "Spit it out!"

"That you use your half of the money to buy one-half interest in Green Springs company."

Dex was jarred. He blinked in astonishment and stared at the seamed, rocky old face. "What're you talking about?"

"I mean just what I said. You can have half the god-damned gold — but only providin' you agree to buy into Green Springs Stage and Transfer Company as my pardner. Now you listen to me: you can pull that trigger any time you want to; I won't budge an inch, and I don't give a damn if you do — hear that, boy? All right; you want the money, and I'm sayin' before these boys here that you can have it. But you got to plough it back into my company — be my pardner in it; and as the pardner, you got to run the company. I'm retired, damn you, and I aim to stay retired. You'll run Green Springs company as half owner. Now, there it is. *You* spit or close the window!"

Dex was flabbergasted. He turned slowly and looked at the four possemen old man Turnbull had brought with him. They were just as nonplussed as he was, and returned his stare as blankly as he stared at them. The man who spoke into the impasse was, strangely enough, John Turnbull. He was wearing the same expressionless look Dex had come to know so well. The only movement he made was to throw his head a little; a quirk of derisive scorn that spoke as loud as his words did.

"Go ahead, Williams; take the old devil up on it. He'll break you, like he broke me. Go ahead! You two've got a lot in common. It's iron up your backs, maybe. I'll look forward to watching this pardnership — and be damned to you both!"

"Well?" the old man said, his bird-bright eyes fixed steadily on Dex. "What's it goin' to be?"

"How about the charges against me?" Dex asked, stalling for more time to marshal his thoughts before the onslaught of confusion the old man had thrown him into.

"Damn the charges against you. I'll fix them if I have to sit up all night for a week with Tom Bulow. You got no worries there."

"And your son?" Dex asked. "What about him?"

The old eyes had a hint of hurt in their depths, but the craggy features didn't give an inch. "If it was just the money — just the robbing of the company — I'd let him go and be damned to him; but there's murder, y'know. A poor devil he didn't even know, and that — that tramp over at the Flats. I can't help him, and wouldn't if I could. Not over murder." He blew out a thick breath. "And I don't want to talk about him again, any more at all." He turned and jerked his head at the blacksmith. "Mike; tie him on his horse and head back. Williams and I'll come along directly."

The possemen seemed glad for the chance to leave. They had young Turnbull tied, and were standing to horse when the blacksmith turned and frowned at the old man. "What about this money, Fred? We could stow that aboard, too."

"Never mind. Williams and I'll fetch it back. Just leave us those saddlebags we brought along."

And that's the way it was. Long after the sound of the others had died out in their passing, Dex and Frederick Turnbull packed the stage loot into saddlebags, tied them behind their saddles, swung up and followed after the others. For Dex it was anti-climax. His body was sore and tired to the point of complete exhaustion, but more than anything else, he was hungry. Ravenously and wolfishly hungry. He thought of Marge and the meals she had brought him while he'd been in jail. He turned toward the old scarecrow riding beside him on the thoroughbred horse and expensive saddle.

"Marge gave you the map all right." It was a statement, not a question.

"Yup. She gave it to me just like you'd drawed it. It wasn't hard to find the cache, but you took so doggoned long in showin' up I was getting jumpy for fear something'd gone wrong. Anyway, I didn't trust you, Williams. Didn't trust you worth a damn."

"I don't blame you, I guess."

Frederick Turnbull eased his horse ahead of Dex on the trail and twisted backwards, looking at the younger man. "Know why I'm making you that proposition, Williams? Because you're my type of a man. You're honest, and you got iron in you. That's all I ask of any man. We'll put the company back on its feet, then I can sit back again. What say, boy?"

Dex shrugged. "I don't know what to say. Listen — I was mad back there. I don't really want half that money. I've got no right to it."

"Hell, man, I know that. I'm giving it to you; get that through your thick skull, will you? Giving it to you so's you'll be able to buy into a big company with a solid bankroll. You won't get a chance like this again in a long time — maybe never. Now, dammit all, I want an answer."

Dex's anger flared at the old man's arrogance. He shot a warm look at the old face. "Back off, Turnbull," he said coldly. "You don't make any demands on me now or any other time; you understand that?"

Quickly Turnbull adopted another tack. "All right, Williams; all right. But how about the girl? How about Will Herndon's daughter? She believes in you, boy. She'll more'n likely marry you if you ask her. What about her?"

"Well; what about her?"

Turnbull smiled craftily. "Give her security, Williams. You can as a pardner in the company. Give her what she deserves, dammit. She's a real soldier, that little lady; a real soldier. She'd a hung right beside you if she could. You won't find many like that. Marry

216

her, and if you won't take half the money —
then by God I'll make you a wedding present
o' half the Green Springs company. *Now* what
d'you say?"

Dex swore softly. "What do you want me
in your company so bad for, Mister Turnbull?"

"Mister hell," the old man shot right back.
"I'm Fred. What's your first name, Williams?"

"Dex. Short for Dexter."

"I should've remembered. All right; I'm
Fred and you're Dex. Dex, I want you in the
company because I want a man running it.
That answer you? I want guts and brains and
iron to take my place. You're the first one
I've seen around Lovell in twenty years that's
got all three. Now, boy, let's forget the un-
pleasantness. I'm begging you to take over.
Will you, Dex?"

"How do you know I've got the brains for
it?"

Fred Turnbull laughed his harsh, grating
laugh. "After the way you out-foxed the
Bulows and John and me, and everybody else,
you ask a question like that? You got brains,
boy, and I'll teach you the ropes. How about
it?"

Dex looked worried. "All right. On one
condition. The first time you snap at me,

Fred, you're either going to get up-ended and get your rear kicked, or you're going to hire a new pardner."

Turnbull yanked up his reins, backed his horse with no regard for the narrowness of the trail and the steepness of the fall on their off-side, and shoved out his injured arm. "Shake, Dex — by God shake. You're the answer to an old man's prayer."

They shook, and afterwards Dex was gloomily silent all the way back to Lovell, but Fred Turnbull wasn't. He had, it seemed, lost a part of himself, and in almost the same breath had found another segment that fitted in exactly where his son had been cast out. And he was that kind of a man, too. Blood meant nothing to him unless it was loyal, honest, rock-hard blood. He was that strange make of a man who valued worth above relationship; the kind of a man who wasn't blind to faults in his bloodline. Hard as granite and as honest as the day was long. A rare, iron breed that is all but extinct, but which did more to settle and tame the wild frontiers of the world than all the guns and soldiers of all the nations combined.

Dex rode into town a little ahead of a thoroughly disgusted, exhausted and disgruntled posse led by Slim Barr, whose hat sat gingerly over a purple welt on top of his head. He rode directly to the sheriff's office and left his horse outside, with orders for it to be taken to the livery barn and grained.

Then he walked, flat-footed, heavily, into the office and looked at the upturned, wan faces that were watching him almost without life in their blank stares. He crossed to the wall-bench, where Will Herndon, dust-caked and pouch-eyed, was slouching, and dropped down. Reaching for his tobacco sack he worried up a slovenly cigarette, leaned into the spluttering match Eb Bulow held out, then smoked a moment under the steady, unyielding glance of Sheriff Tom Bulow.

"Well, it's over, fellers," he said dully. "That blacksmith at the north end of town is bringing John Turnbull in. Fred Turnbull has the money, and that's about all there is to tell."

Tom Bulow spoke softly around the smoke that drifted up past his eyes from the cigarette dangling from the corner of his mouth. "We've already got John in a cell. He come in about an hour ago."

"Oh," Dex said absently, "then you probably know about it."

"We heard," Will said. "Dex, why didn't you wait? I'd of been back."

"Didn't dare, Will. Figured to, until I heard about John killin' that woman. After that, I

219

was afraid he'd run off, and if he had, I'd of been an outlaw for life. Who'd of believed what we suspected John of, after he was gone?" Dex smoked a moment, then went on again in his tired, listless voice. "I was scairt stiff. It was bad, the way I had to do it. The old man shot me once. I had no way of knowin' whether he'd do what Marge told him to or not. If he hadn't — well — he did, so that's that."

"Yeah," Tom Bulow said placidly; then he got up and crossed the room and shoved out his hand. "I'm sorry, Dex. Sorry as all outdoors."

Dex took the hard grip and pumped it once, then let it go. Eb Bulow was next; only he, being younger and less grave, had a saturine little smile on his face.

"Me, too, Dex. Lord, I'm almost glad you stuck that knife in my belly, that time. No hard feelings?"

"No." Dex worked up a little answering smile. "Where's Slim? I'd like to tell him why I took him on that wild goose chase."

Will shifted position on the hard bench. There was a little twinkle in his face, like there was in the blue eyes of the sheriff. "Slim said he was goin' out and get drunk, son. Said he never misjudged a man so badly in his life."

"Well, if I didn't feel so damn used up,"

Dex said dryly, "doggoned if I wouldn't go hunt him up and get drunk with him."

Will stood up and slapped his hat against his coat. The dust flew. "Naw; you'd better come home with me. Marge's waiting with supper."

As though reminded of something, Dex stood up and ran a hand over the back of his neck. "Say, I'm half owner of the Green Springs Stage and Transfer Company. I reckon I forgot to mention that."

"You're what?" Will Herndon said.

Dex looked apologetic. "Half owner of the stage company."

"I heard you," Will said; then he looked around the room at the others and saw the same blank astonishment in their faces, and made a dolorous shake of his head. "I'll be totally damned. Well — see you later, fellers. Come on, Dex, let's go home."

They went, and Will didn't speak again until Marge met them at the door and ran into Dex's arms with a small cry. He cleared his throat and looked embarrassed when his daughter kissed Dex right there in front of him.

"Well — honey — can't you wait? You got to do a thing like that right here on the stoop, with the whole doggoned town watching?"

He pushed them both inside, flung a red-faced look outside before he slammed the door, then rammed his pockets full of balled-up hands and rocked back on his heels, staring at them both. "Now what, Dex?"

"Think I'd better get married," Dex said so matter-of-factly that Will look horrified, and Marge broke out into sudden laughter. When she stifled the noise, she took his hand and tugged him toward the kitchen.

"Honey, hadn't you better wash up and eat supper first?"

He looked down into the luminous beauty of her dark eyes and grinned slowly; then laughed aloud and turned toward Will, who was watching them with an expression that was equal parts of pride and pure embarrassment. "Will, do you mind?"

"Well, before supper I sure as hell do, but after we eat I'm at your disposition, young man."

They all three laughed.

Lauran Paine who, under his own name and various pseudonyms has written over 900 books, was born in Duluth, Minnesota, a descendant of the Revolutionary War patriot and author, Thomas Paine. His family moved to California when he was at an early age and his apprenticeship as a Western writer came about through the years he spent in the livestock trade, rodeos, and even motion pictures where he served as an extra because of his expert horsemanship in several films starring movie cowboy Johnny Mack Brown. In the late 1930s, Paine trapped wild horses in northern Arizona and even, for a time, worked as a professional farrier. Paine came to know the Old West through the eyes of many who had been born in the previous century and he learned that Western life had been very different from the way it was portrayed on the screen. "I knew men who had killed other men," he later recalled. "But they were the exceptions. Prior to and during the Depression, people were just too busy eking out an existence to indulge in Saturday-night brawls." He served in the U.S. Navy in the Second World War and began writing for Western pulp magazines following his discharge. It is interesting to note that all of his earliest novels (written under his own name and the pseudonym Mark Carrel) were published in the British market and he soon had as strong a following in that country as in the United States. Paine's Western fiction is characterized by strong plots, authenticity, an apparently effortless ability to construct situation and character, and a preference for building his stories upon a solid foundation of historical fact. ADOBE EMPIRE (1956), one of his best novels, is a fictionalized account of the last twenty years in the life of trader William Bent and, in an off-trail way, has a melancholy, bittersweet texture that is not easily forgotten. MOON PRAIRIE (1950), first published in the United States in 1994, is a memorable story set during the mountain man period of the frontier. In later novels such as THE HOMESTEADERS (1986) or THE OPEN RANGE MEN (1990), he showed that the special magic and power of his stories and characters had only matured along with his basic themes of changing times, changing attitudes, learning from experience, respecting nature, and the yearning for a simpler, more moderate way of life.